Ride Out The Storm

Ride Out The

Storm

MARGARET E. BELL

WILLIAM MORROW & CO. · NEW YORK · 1951

Ride Out The Storm

CHAPTER   1

LISBETH RAN UPSTAIRS two steps at a time with Billy the Third bounding past her. Her thumping and the sharp rap of the fawn's hoofs made the downstairs hallway echo like a boat shop. Lisbeth heard Mother exclaim, "Mercy!" but she gave it no thought, because she was in a tremendous hurry. Long Paul had said he would put Turk's-heads on her new oars and help her get her boat in, and it was already late. She was soaking wet, as a dribbling trail of water on the stairway testified. At the foot of the stairs her water spaniel, old Doggie Dash, shook himself and sat down to wait.

Billy reached the upstairs hall first, as he always did, and with a few abrupt and violent movements sent the water flying from his thick coat. Then he sniffed at the floor and, with his long ears pointed forward, turned and walked gracefully through the open door of Robert's room.

"Come on out of there," Lisbeth coaxed, going to her own room at the front of the house. "Robbie isn't there. He won't be home till June. Come on, Billy. Come on!"

You always had to wheedle a deer. Dad said they couldn't be taught and she guessed they really couldn't. Billy was last year's fawn, and instead of growing less capricious he was growing more so.

Lisbeth worked her feet out of her wet sneakers, pulled off her socks, and hung them on a wire she had rigged back of the stovepipe. When she had got out of her dripping sweater and her T shirt, she found a bath towel and rubbed her mop of red hair as dry as she could. Then she took the sweater and leaned out of the window to wring it out. She could see the squall that had soaked her moving on across Hermit Bay under its black cloud, leaving the cannery roofs steaming in the sun.

Lisbeth loved April, with the sun mounting high in the sky again and the days growing long. Some

Aprils were cold, and you kept on wearing your wool underwear until nearly the end of the month, but this one was a warm April. The snow line had already melted up to a thousand feet above the beach.

She shook the sweater, and then she saw Dad coming along the boardwalk from the new store where his office was. Behind him were the cannery buildings at the edge of the bay, and the bunkhouse and the mess hall. On the other side of the walk the wild forest with its border of salmonberry bushes came down to end abruptly at the rocky beach. On the big tides the green water of the bay covered the rocks under the walk and rose to the twisted roots of the trees themselves.

The Craig house stood on a mossy point that projected a short distance into the bay. Behind it and beyond it the dark forest rose on the mountainsides to the even mark of the snow line. Lisbeth saw that the peaks stood out white and sharp against the deep blue of the sky. The clouds were gone. She drew back, knowing that Dad must be coming home for tea and that meant it was almost four o'clock. There was no time to lose.

She had put on dry jeans and a flannel shirt and was trying to tie the laces of a dry pair of sneakers, with Billy nibbling at them, when she heard Mother's voice say distinctly, "She's thirteen, Alex. We can't let her grow up so . . . well . . . so wild and unused to the company of cultivated girls."

"It isn't cultivated girls I'm worrying about," Dad's voice replied. "It's character that counts in this world—counts more now than it ever did. Young as she is, she's got more. . . ."

"But, Dad, we can't keep her from growing up. The world is changing. She'll have to be a woman in it—in a different world from ours. There simply aren't any pioneers any more. She must be prepared for a different life from this."

The voices from downstairs in the living room carried clearly up the stovepipe, and Lisbeth paused and let the fawn chew her shoelace as she leaned forward, listening. They were talking again about sending her away to school.

"Oh, I know! There's no place left where a man's his own man the way it used to be here in Alaska. I know we must send her to school." Dad's voice was bitter, as it always was when he referred to the restrictions on a man's freedom. "But let's look at this school well. I don't trust these schools with their modern ideas of daubing paint instead of learning Latin. Supposing she comes home again with an ambition to be a cover girl or . . . or . . . one of those female crooners!"

"Now, Dad," Mother's voice soothed, "that school we chose last year is a good one. It's not too modern and not too old-fashioned. This year she really must go. It's wrong to let her grow up so unprepared for the outside world."

Lisbeth felt a pang of guilt because she was eavesdropping. Hastily she tied her shoe and slipped noiselessly downstairs, leaving Billy to nose about her room with his endless curiosity. He would soon go downstairs to beg for a lump of sugar at the tea table. She tried to banish from her mind the words of doom she had just heard. She went out through the kitchen with Doggie Dash at her heels, closed the door softly behind her, and walked slowly to the shed at the rear of the house.

She had promised. That was the worst of it. Last year, she had promised that if they would give her one more year she would go without fussing. A year had seemed so long then, but now, suddenly, it was half gone. She would have May, June, July, and August, and what was left of this April. And then? She was shaken and heavyhearted at the thought of leaving Hermit Bay.

In the shed she took her newly varnished oars off

the rack where they had dried. With them over her shoulder and Doggie Dash at her heels, she went around the house and down the long boardwalk to the cannery. There was no use thinking about it, she told herself. But she couldn't stop. She had seen the world outside and she didn't like it. She would never live in it—no, never!—no matter how well they prepared her for it. If the pioneers were gone, she would be a hermit like the old hermit of Hermit Bay and live in a log cabin up in the Narrow Arm.

When Robert had finished school, the Craigs and Uncle Jim had gone down to California for his graduation. Lisbeth could still remember the dreadful crowds. It all came back to her now with sickening vividness—the confusion of dressed-up people pushing and milling around afterwards, chattering and laughing. She remembered clinging to Dad's hand, because Dad was quiet, while all of Robbie's friends crowded around Uncle Jim. Uncle Jim had a way with him. All sorts of people admired him— the men at the cannery, the Indians, and the people at Robbie's school.

Now Robbie was away at college. He had been gone two winters and one summer, to make up for the year when the salmon run failed and there had been no money to send him out. He would be changed again when he came home in June. She knew he would, because she could remember how he had changed after his first year away from home a long time ago. It had taken her days to get over being shy with him. And now she, Lisbeth, would have no more winters at home, not for years and years.

Lisbeth looked around her—at the golden yellow of the April seaweed on the rocks, at the pale-green tips of new growth on the hemlock, and at the wind-ruffled water of the bay. She looked up at the high white peaks of the mountains carved against the limpid blue of the sky. Today, more than ever before, she was aware of her deep feeling for her home, because she was doomed to change, and her country, her beloved Alaska, must somehow change also. There would be no more pioneers, because there would be more and more regulations and rigmaroles. She had heard Dad say so. But, worst of all, she realized deep within herself that it was she who would change most, and in changing she would somehow lose her companionship with the forest and the animals and birds and with the weather itself. She knew that afterward nothing would be the same. This was her last April.

In front of Dad's office she turned and walked up

the ramp to the cannery buildings. They were quiet now, because the packing season would not begin until August. Only the old-timers were in the bunkhouse and they were getting the boats ready for the season. The rest of the crew would come when the season began. There were not many sailormen left who could make Turk's-heads and tighten them properly on an oar, but Long Paul was one of them. He could do anything that needed doing on a boat. He had been with the Craigs for so many years that nobody could remember being without him. This year he was skipper on their new packer, the *Vega*. He was Lisbeth's truest and most valued friend. He never talked much, but he always knew the important things to talk about, like what phase of the moon it was or when the next minus tides would be, or certain observations about life that Lisbeth remembered.

She ran across the wharf with Dash beside her, and together they looked down at the *Vega*. "Paul!" she called. "Long Paul, are you there?"

The wheelhouse door opened and Long Paul came out, with a marlinespike and the two Turk's-heads in his hand. He was six feet and three inches tall and as skinny as a rope. Once Ole had threatened to tie up the pile driver with Long Paul for a hawser, and the joke had never been forgotten. Paul's hands and face were weathered to the color of hemp, and the shock of bristling hair that thrust itself out under the peak of his cap was like the frayed end of a hawser. His eyes, deep-set in his creased face, were light blue, with furrows fanning to his temples at either side. He came up the ladder with his stubby pipe in his mouth.

With the pipe gripped in his teeth he said, "I begin to think you got stuck on a reef somewheres."

"I almost did," Lisbeth answered, her eyes on the two intricate circles of rope in his hand. She had an impulse to tell Paul her secret, but she could not. When you said things in words they became more real, and she didn't want this to be real—not until it had to be. "I got caught up the beach in that squall," she explained.

"Ya," said Paul. "It was a wet one."

"Look at my oars, Paul. Aren't they fine? They're light as can be. Feel them." She held the oars up proudly.

Paul pulled his long body over the stringer that ran along the face of the wharf. "Good," he said, hefting an oar with his free hand.

They went together to the door of the big empty warehouse and Lisbeth slid it back. Her skiff was there, with its new coat of bright red paint. A coil of white halibut cord hung on a nail near it. Lisbeth got the cord and they pulled a sawhorse out in the sun and sat there to work on the oars with the old dog at their feet. Lisbeth knew how to wrap oars, but she could not pull the cord tight enough to withstand the scraping of the oarlocks. She watched as Long Paul skillfully turned the oar in his brown hands and wound the white cord in place.

"If we get through in time we can get the skiff in, can't we, Paul?" she asked.

"If Ole get here in time we can," he told her. He finished the wrapping and slipped one of the rope circles over the oar, letting it slide down to where the wrapping ended. Then he began to tighten it with the marlinespike. Round and round he went until the strands of fine rope were snug on the oar and crisscrossed like a Turk's turban.

"That's beautiful," Lisbeth said admiringly. "It looks so expert."

When both were done, they made neat guards that would keep her oars from slipping through the oarlocks if she let go the handles. "Oh, thank you, Paul," she cried. "I'm so proud of them. It isn't every girl has a pair of Turk's-heads on her oars!"

"It is not every girl needs 'em," Paul remarked.

"I bet every girl would like to have them just the same," Lisbeth said confidently.

Long Paul snorted. "Most girls never seen a pair oars in their life," he told her.

Lisbeth returned his look gravely. "Never?" she asked incredulously. As long as she could remember, she had had a pair of oars. As she grew, Dad had got her longer oars and bigger boats until now, at thirteen, she had seven-and-a-half-footers and a twelve-foot skiff. And she was going away to live for months and months among girls who had never seen a pair of oars! She jumped to her feet.

"Let's put the boat in," she said quickly. "I'll haul on one side."

"Take it easy," her companion advised. "You want to scrape that nice copper paint off her bottom?" He paused and they could hear the hollow sound of steps coming between the two buildings.

Dash got up, stretched himself, and walked to the corner of the warehouse to investigate. In a moment Ole came out on the wharf with his energetic, springy step. Lisbeth started to speak, but Ole did not even look their way. He walked across the wharf hurriedly to where an old piece of hawser lay stretched out in the sun.

He bent over it with a hand on each knee, looking

at it intently. "Hey! Long Paul! What is wrong?" he cried in mock excitement, reaching down and shaking the thick rope. Then he straightened up and looked around at them. "By gar, Paul," he exclaimed, "that hawser give me a scare! I thought it was you." He looked back at the rope. "Who tie the knot in the end of that rope? Make it look yust like Long Paul." He winked at Lisbeth and she could not help laughing, even though they usually carried on their jokes with apparent seriousness.

"Oh, that old yoke!" Long Paul jeered. "Youse ain't got wits to think up a new one."

Ole was younger than Long Paul. He was broader in build and very fair of skin and hair. He was shy and blushed easily, but Lisbeth understood shyness and Ole was always jolly and playful with her. She could remember when he used to carry her on his big shoulder when she was a very little girl. Next to Long Paul she loved Ole most of all her friends.

"You'll help us get the skiff in, won't you, Ole?" she asked.

"Ya. I halp," Ole replied. "You been my boss over ten year now. I halp."

The two men caught hold of the skiff, one on each side, and started across the wharf to the slip. They staggered along, each accusing the other of having grown so puny and weak that he was worthless. Lisbeth followed, with the oars on her shoulder and Dash at her heels. They went down the slip to the float and launched the skiff without a splash. Lisbeth praised the job and climbed into the boat with Dash after her.

"I t'ink you have to fire Long Paul end of summer," Ole said, pushing her off. "He is getting too old to work."

"We'll pension him," Lisbeth answered, "and let him sit in the sun and make Turk's-heads." She placed the oarlocks and set her oars.

"Ya," Long Paul agreed. "Then with me off the yob Ole will not know which way the wind blows even."

With the two of them watching her, Lisbeth feathered oars smoothly and rowed away. She turned out around the face of the dock and headed up the bay. There was a high point of land only a half mile beyond her house. Around this point was the Narrow Arm, where the old hermit for whom the bay had been named had lived and died many years ago. The ruins of his log cabin were still there, overgrown now with gray currant and alder. As soon as she rounded the point, she let her oars slide out and rest on their new guards, while she placed a board across the gunwales in the stern. Sitting on the board, she could face the bow and push on the oars instead of pulling. Then she could watch the shore and the water ahead of her. On this side of the point she was out of view of the cannery. Even the end of the wharf was out of sight. It was like being far away in a wilderness where no man save the old hermit had ever set foot or plied an oar.

Here the high wooded promontory sheltered an arm of the bay that reached for almost half a mile into the woods. It was no more than a hundred yards wide and so was called the Narrow Arm. For Lisbeth it was an enchanted spot, a place where she could watch the otter and the mink, the seal and the eagle. Up the creek at the end of the Narrow Arm she had seen beaver and marten. Ravens circled over the forest and the red-breasted sapsuckers flashed in the trees. In May small birds came to nest in the brush at the forest's edge. On one side of the Arm there were grassy flats with sandspits reaching out into the clear salt water. On the other side the forest grew down steeply to the very limits of the tide. Here seaweed, carried on the big tides, still clung to the lower branches of the cedar trees, and goosetongue and beach grass grew in the seams of the rocks. The tide ran free in the deep tapering channel until it spread itself over a white pebble beach where the creek came in.

Lisbeth loved this place with a deep and incommunicable love. She knew each moss-covered windfall along the edge of the forest, each stump where she could sit and wait for the birds to come near, the big rock where she could hide and watch the otter fishing and eating their fish. Best of all was the beaver dam up the stream in the alders. Sometimes in midsummer she would lie on her back on the sandspit where the paintbrush grew, eating wild strawberries and dreaming. She had built a little fireplace on the sandspit where she could make tea, and she always had a waterproof grub box in her skiff. She spent hours and hours in the Narrow Arm.

On this day in April, she rowed past the sandspit so close in that her oars touched bottom and stirred the sand into little whirls like whirls of smoke in the clear water. On the opposite side where the channel was deep, a seal, swimming with his head up, looked at her curiously and sank down again with hardly a ripple of water. When an otter dove you could see his back as he curved to go down, but a seal's head simply sank out of sight. In a moment her seal was there again, sliding easily through the water, disappearing and reappearing but keeping even with her boat all the time. Any other day Lisbeth would have spoken to him, or she might have crossed the Narrow Arm and stood on the high rocks on the other side where she could see him swimming under the water. But today her face was grave and preoccupied and every now and then she stopped rowing and sat drifting in the eddy, lost in thought.

Paul's remark that most girls knew nothing about oars and boats had awakened unbearable doubts. At a girls' school there would be no room for the sort of thing in which she excelled: tracking wild animals in the woods, where she could distinguish the tracks of the marten from the mink, the otter from the beaver as easily as reading her A B C's; making tea in the pouring rain; scenting a bear in the dense forest. She sniffed, thinking of it, because the mother bears were out of hibernation now with their tiny cubs. A breeze drifted offshore and for a moment she thought she detected the musky smell, sharper than skunk but not as unpleasant as mink or raven. Dad said bears smelled something like pigs but not quite. Lisbeth had never smelled pigs.

She watched the edge of the timber but nothing moved, and her doleful thoughts continued. At school none of these things would matter. There would be tennis and golf and horseback riding because there was nothing better to do. She would never kneel down to drink from a cold spring or lie in the deep moss dreaming.

With aching heart, she vowed to try to face things squarely. She had known few people. From her one trip to the States she remembered not individuals but crowds. Toward people in the mass she felt a vague hostility and an indefinable fear. When tourists flocked off the ships that came in to load salmon at the Craig cannery, only Lisbeth's eagerness to see the captain kept her from taking to the woods to avoid the curious eyes and the ever-present cameras. It was like an invasion from the outside world, this rush of well-dressed strangers with questions about ordinary things that everybody knew. Were the bears really dangerous? Were the "pines" so dense all over the coast? Every evergreen tree was a pine to them. Actually there were no pines at all in the forest of Hermit Bay. It was a forest of cedar, hemlock, and spruce, but city people couldn't tell them apart. Someone always asked, "Don't you get lonely, little girl?"

Why, the hours of the day were never long enough. You never had quite enough of each season before it changed into the next. The long days of summer would change all too soon to the short days of winter, when you would hear the wolf chorus and know that never, never could such exciting and eerily beautiful sounds come from anywhere except nature herself. These tourists called it howling, without ever having heard it. Lisbeth's revulsion contained an element of fear because, to her, outsiders seemed to be all alike and all alien. As she tried to picture in her mind just what her arrival at school would be like, she thought of the commencement crowd at Robert's school.

"I'll never be able to get through it," she said desperately, as tears suddenly gushed out of her eyes.

She dropped her oars and impatiently blew her nose. Then she rowed on slowly toward the white beach at the end of the Arm. Ahead of her swam two small ducks, trailing perfect V's on the smooth water. Gradually she felt the quiet seeping into her, the April quiet that was waiting for the songbirds to return and the first flowers to open their petals. She loved the firsts—Johnny-jump-ups for spring, the first wild strawberries for summer, and the snowflakes for winter. All of nature's announcements of her changing seasons she awaited with a sort of mystical attentiveness, as though they were religious rites. She was filled with wonder at the detailed and

varied beauty of a wilderness where new discoveries
never ended.

It did not occur to her that if she were one of the
wild animals, as she sometimes imagined herself to
be, she would not be aware of this beauty nor of the
mysticism apparent in it. Lisbeth felt the wonder
of nature as she herself was part of it, but thinking
about it made her doubtful and frightened lest she
lose her wonderful world.

Because her life was taken up with the natural
world around her, she read very little, for the most
part only those books that were required in the
courses of her correspondence school. But she studied faithfully and always managed to get her lessons
in the mail in time for the boat that came from
Juneau every Saturday. Those lessons were the price
she had gladly paid for being permitted to stay at
home.

As she approached the white pebble beach, the
evening song of a wood thrush poured joyously out
of the trees just beyond the ruins of the old hermit's
cabin. She stopped rowing and listened. The first
songbird had arrived! April's first thrush!

C H A P T E R 2

ON THE DAY in June when Robert's message came
through on the Craigs' receiving set, saying that he
had arrived and was flying out from Juneau, Lisbeth
was sitting in a cedar tree in the Narrow Arm. She
was watching Mrs. Higgenbottom, a big brown bear,
fishing for crabs for her cubs. Lisbeth was beginning
to fidget, because the tide had started in and it was
time for the Higgenbottoms to go back to the woods.
The cubs, Castor and Pollux, were pretty well filled
up and had ceased to get underfoot, as the mother
bear turned over the rocks and pawed among the

seaweed. Yet the old bear continued to hunt out crabs and eat them herself. Lisbeth's seat on the sloping limb of the cedar tree was safe enough, but it was not very comfortable. Much as she admired the Higgenbottom family, she always grew a little uneasy when they failed to depart for the woods at the turn of the tide.

She had left her boat down by the point and commanded Dash to remain in it. The old dog was used to the routine now, because Lisbeth had discovered the Higgenbottoms in May, when the cubs were merely woolly balls of fur. Since this was Lisbeth's first opportunity to observe brown bears, she had spent many hours watching them during the minus tides. Between the point and the sandspit there was a weedy beach that sloped down like a shovel scoop turned towards the woods. When the low tide reached minus one or more, only a few inches of water remained in the lower end of the shovel, where small crabs sheltered themselves under the seaweed to await the return of the tide.

On the day when Lisbeth first saw the bear and her cubs, she had just rowed around the point, sitting on the board and facing forward as was her custom. The bear was there, turning over the rocks and seaweed, looking for crabs. Lisbeth had stopped rowing and stared. She had never seen a brown bear in the Narrow Arm before. At first she did not see the cubs, so well did they blend in with the rocks and weeds. But when they came forward to see what new delicacy their mother had discovered for them, they got cuffed for their pains, and then there was such a commotion of fur rolling this way and that and such a squealing that Lisbeth sat wide-eyed with wonder, murmuring, "Oh . . . oh," over and over. Brown bears had been seen on the flats away up at the head of the main bay, where the big river came in and where Lisbeth was not permitted to go alone. She had never expected to see such a wonderful sight right here in the Narrow Arm. She was well aware of the fearlessness and the ferocity of the brownies and she knew it was wise to give them a wide berth. On that day she had watched from her boat until the mother bear retreated from the incoming tide and ambled back to the shelter of the woods, with her two cubs hiking along behind her. As Lisbeth rowed homeward, she named the bears and incorporated them into the large company of wild creatures she had seen and would keep in her memory.

When the big tides were over and the lower end of the beach no longer was drained of its water, Mrs.

Higgenbottom and her twins did not appear in the Narrow Arm. It was then that Lisbeth ventured ashore and discovered the old cedar just above the spot where the bears fished for crab. It was a venerable old tree, its long sweeping branches draped with tawny moss. She found that by driving a few spikes for hand- and footholds in the lower trunk, she could get up into the tree. With her perch prepared high in the old cedar, she impatiently awaited the next minus tides. Then she went early to the spot and, safe in her tree, watched for Mrs. Higgenbottom and Castor and Pollux to arrive. She kept all this secret, because she feared that if Dad knew that she was venturing so close to the haunt of a brown bear, he would not permit her to do it.

So on this June day Lisbeth, from her perch in the cedar tree, saw the plane circle and turn in to the wind to come down. She knew it might very well be Robert coming home, but she dared not get down with the bears so close at hand. The tide was coming in now, and she expected Mrs. Higgenbottom to give up and go back to the woods as usual, using the trail she and the cubs had beaten down through the high grass above the beach. But as the tide came farther in and covered her fishing ground, the old bear walked only a few paces up the beach and then lay down and rolled in the seaweed. The cubs, who had grown from mere furry balls into bear shapes, began to wrestle, standing up on their hind legs and pushing each other around. Lisbeth watched with mixed feelings of pleasure and anxiety. She watched Mrs. Higgenbottom cool herself in the seaweed and then get up and absently lick her left foreleg. Lisbeth craned her neck to look through the branches and make sure that Dash had remained in the boat, and saw with relief that he was lying on the stern seat, apparently asleep. Mrs. Higgenbottom looked around her for a moment and then walked slowly with her long velvet strides to the very tree where Lisbeth was perched high up in the branches. When she reached the shade, the old bear lay down with a comfortable grunt, while her twins continued their romp.

Up on the sloping limb Lisbeth felt suddenly insecure. She threw her arms around the trunk of the tree, clutching it with all her might, while the strength seemed to drain out of her joints. All sorts of possibilities flashed through her mind as she clung to the tree. The brownies were known to be particularly ferocious when guarding their young. Not a year passed when some homesteader or hunter was not mauled or killed by a brown bear. Lisbeth was in a fix and she knew it. It was almost suppertime, even though the sun was still high in the sky. If Mrs. Higgenbottom had decided to spend the night here, she would be treed until Dad came looking for her with his gun. Lisbeth was proud of her ability to take care of herself. To have to be rescued was too humiliating to contemplate and, besides, she didn't want Mrs. Higgenbottom shot at, even if it were only to scare her. No one had fired a gun in the Narrow Arm as long as the Craigs had been in Hermit Bay. But worse still was the almost certain possibility that Dash would grow nervous if she did not come back to the skiff in the usual time. She could see him now, sitting up as he waited for her in the boat. If he caught sight of Castor and Pollux romping so near her tree, he might get it into his head that he should come and drive them away. Mrs. Higgenbottom would make short work of an old dog like Dash.

Lisbeth tried to compose herself and think things out. She might try making a noise, in the hope it would scare Mrs. Higgenbottom away. But there was the chance that the old lady would get stubborn or curious instead of scared. Peering down through the branches, she could get glimpses of the big bear, who apparently was taking a snooze. It was quite a while before Lisbeth's heart stopped pounding and she could relax her grip on the tree without feeling that she would slide down the long limb into the very arms of her erstwhile friend. Then came the thing she dreaded most—an outburst of barking down the beach.

Instantly the big bear was on her feet. She walked out from under the tree and stared with her near-sighted eyes in the direction of the noise. Lisbeth could see Dash coming toward her on the run. He was bravely setting out to attempt to drive off the bears and rescue her. The two cubs stopped romping and watched their mother. Mrs. Higgenbottom had spotted the dog and started out to meet him. She would kill Dash! She would kill the brave old dog without half trying.

"Mrs. Higgenbottom!" Lisbeth shrieked. "Don't go after Dash! He's an old dog. Mrs. Higgenbottom, please come back!" Lisbeth screamed helplessly, "Come back—come back—come back!"

At her first shriek, Mrs. Higgenbottom came to a stop so suddenly that she slid a little way in the sand. Lisbeth followed up this gain with more screaming entreaties. The bear seemed quite unnerved by the shrieking that came from she knew not where. She turned away from the oncoming dog and reached her cubs in two strides. Giving each of them a swift spank with her big forepaw, she sent them bounding for the woods.

At that same moment Lisbeth heard the roar of Robert's speedboat. "Go it! Go it, Mrs. Higgenbottom!" she yelled, fearful lest Dad arrive with a gun.

Dash was under the tree now, panting and bristling at the same time. Castor and Pollux had vanished into the woods, and the mother bear stood for a moment gazing back at the scene of the disturbance. Then she seemed to melt into the brush and disappear.

Lisbeth looked toward the point where the motor boat had cut a wide fan of white water as she came around into the Narrow Arm. The roar of the motor diminished and then stopped, as the boat came into the shallow water. Silence again filled the wilderness. There was not the crack of a twig nor the stir of a branch to tell that danger had passed that way.

Trembling, and hoarse from screaming, Lisbeth dropped down to the ground. She threw her arms around old Doggie Dash. "You old silly!" she scolded him. "You're too old to be brave any more." She hugged him and stroked his head.

Then with surprise and relief she heard her brother's voice. "Lisbeth! You crazy kid! Come on! That was a brown bear. I haven't got a gun."

As Lisbeth walked with shaky knees down the beach to meet him, it seemed like old times and she wondered if he would be cross. When he was a boy and she was a little girl, he had often been furious when she wandered too far and he had to hunt for her. She was astonished at how tall he was. He was dressed in not too clean cords and an old leather jacket, and his blond hair was as wild as it always had been, but he was different. Besides being so tall he was different.

"Why, Robbie!" she exclaimed, trying to hide the traces of fear by shouting louder than was necessary. "I thought it was Dad in your boat. I'm glad it's you. You came in that plane, didn't you?"

He came up to her, looking toward the forest as he came. "Listen, little wild girl," he said, giving her a keen look, "that bear had you treed, didn't he?"

"That was Mrs. Higgenbottom," Lisbeth said. "I . . . I just happened to be up in the tree."

Her brother burst out laughing. "You're impossible! You've grown but not changed."

He's changed, Lisbeth thought, but not in the way

I guessed. "Did you travel in those duds?" she asked, ignoring his teasing. CO. SCHOOLS

C271017

"Certainly," he replied, his blue eyes brimming with amusement. He looked again at the forest before going on. "And now do you mind telling me how it happened you took up tree sitting? Dad and Mother will be interested, you know."

"I suppose I'll have to tell them now," Lisbeth said reluctantly. "I didn't know it had got so late. I wasn't treed by the bear . . . exactly."

"Then my eyes deceived me," said Robbie. "When I came, you were in a tree and the bear was just leaving. Brief me on what came before that and I'll consider supporting your cause."

"There really isn't anything to it," she told him. "I climbed the tree to wait for Mrs. Higgenbottom and her two cubs to come and fish for crabs. . . ."

"Holy mackerel!" her brother exclaimed. "How are we going to defend such a position when all our lives we've been warned to stay clear of brown bears and even black bears with cubs?"

They walked on slowly, talking as they went. "I was clear of them," Lisbeth insisted. "It was just that today she decided to take a snooze under my tree. Dash caught sight of the cubs and started out to drive them off. I yelled like a banshee, and I suppose she heard the sound of your motor, too. Anyway, she decided it wasn't worth the chance and went back to the woods the way she always has done before today."

They were at the speedboat now, and Robbie pulled it up for her to climb in. "I'm so glad you came," she said. "I was awfully scared for Dash."

"Never mind, little wild girl," he said soothingly. "Heaven protects the likes of you. If I hadn't come, a thunderbolt would have."

Lisbeth sat down on the leather seat in the cockpit with her dog beside her. It was Robbie's talk that was different. That was it. He talked so easily. He hadn't used to.

When the motor was roaring and they were flying along with her skiff in tow, she stole glances at him. He caught her at it and smiled, and Lisbeth felt suddenly shy. It seemed to her he had grown awfully old in two years. Robbie was grown-up now. She felt a little awe-struck and sad. He had called her "wild girl" and she had not called him something back. There was a sort of shimmering distance between them now, the distance between childhood and youth. Robert had crossed over into a place where she was reluctant to go.

Lisbeth was glad that everybody talked at once when they got in the house. Robbie made such fun of his little wild girl sitting in a cedar tree that the whole experience turned out to be a joke. Supper started off merrily. Lisbeth had always known that the best way to hide your secrets was to cover them up with jokes. You just couldn't let your parents know everything about you, no matter how much you loved them. There were certain things they were too old to understand. They would never be able to understand that Castor and Pollux and Mrs. Higgenbottom were dear to her even if they were dangerous, and that she was not afraid of them the way she was afraid of people. Robbie was being light and humorous about everything, and she wondered if he were hiding some secret himself.

Mother kept looking at him fondly and proudly. "I'm so glad you're home again, Robbie," she said. "I think we get rather solemn when you're away."

"But, Mother, we have fun being solemn," Lisbeth protested. "Not that I'm not glad Robbie is home," she added.

In the laughter that followed, Robert said, "You're right, Lisbeth. But when you get outside among the giggling girls, you'd better learn to do as the Romans do."

"What do the Romans do?" she asked.

"It doesn't matter what they do," Dad declared from behind what remained of the roast. "Be what you are and never run with the crowd. You're not a sheep." He turned to Robbie. "Sister's going out to have a look at the world. She'll begin with this school. Later on she can travel if she wants to."

Lisbeth hoped the talk would veer away from school. She grew uneasy every time the subject came up. She remained silent and there was a pause.

Then Mother explained. " 'Do as the Romans do' is just a phrase, Lisbeth. It means that when one goes to a strange place, it's best to watch people and act in accordance with their customs."

"Even if you don't like their customs?" Lisbeth asked.

Mother, Dad, and Robbie all replied to her question at the same time and each said a different thing. Lisbeth thought that very funny and she laughed with them. Mother said something about good manners, and Robbie said something about intelligent adaptation, but it was Dad's advice she listened to. He said, "Wherever you are, be yourself. You'll get on according to what you are worth." She wasn't sure what this meant but it sounded important. It raised a question. What was she worth?

"That's rugged advice, Dad," Robert said. "The catch in it is, what do you mean by getting on?"

Lisbeth had got up to carry the plates out, and now she waited with a plate in either hand for Dad's answer.

Dad hesitated, looking at his son. Then he said, "By getting on, I mean surviving the experiences of this life and keeping your character intact." He gave a little embarrassed laugh. "That sounds pretty pompous in the saying. It's one of those things that don't fit easily into words."

Lisbeth walked slowly to the kitchen and put the plates on the drainboard. When she came back for more plates, Robbie jumped up to help her.

"Don't look so serious, little wild girl," he said.

It was hard to talk back to Robbie's banter. How could he know that she had a tremendous feeling about being worth something? Dad was right. You were worth something in your own right whether other people thought so or not. She decided to change the subject.

"You're going to like the dessert," she told him as they cleared the table. "It's salmonberry fluff. I picked the berries myself this morning." She went into the pantry and brought out a big bowl filled with creamy pudding in which red salmonberries, each as big as half an eggshell, lay encrusted in sugar. "Mother invented it last summer," she said proudly, as she carried it in to the table.

"You mean Mother created it," Robbie told her, as he followed with the pudding dishes.

"You're being pompous," she replied.

"Hear! Hear!" Robbie cried. "The little wild girl learns fast."

"I'm not wild," Lisbeth said impatiently. She was suddenly tired of Robbie's teasing.

"Oh, yes, you are!" he declared. "Isn't she, Mother? It's high time she got out to school."

"School isn't such a bugaboo as it seems," Mother said. "Lisbeth will get on well at school."

Up until now school had not been discussed. It had merely been alluded to once or twice as something understood. Lisbeth felt now that the spell had been broken, that the change was already setting in, like the tide, like something you couldn't stop.

"I hate school!" she cried with a fury she couldn't control. "I don't want even to talk about it. I *hate* it!"

Angry and ashamed, she ran from the table and fled up the stairs to her own room. She was spoiling Robbie's home-coming, but she couldn't help it.

Breathing hard and trying not to cry, she stood staring out of her window, twisting her handkerchief in hands that trembled. She could hear low voices in the dining room. Then she heard a step on the stair, a tap on the door as it opened, and her brother's voice.

"Lisbeth, I didn't mean to be a brute. School is tough to take at first. But, as Mother says, it's not as bad as it seems."

Lisbeth continued to stare out at the huge shadow of the mountain across the bay.

After a moment of silence Robbie went on. "I can't eat a salmonberry in my unforgiven state. Come on down and have dessert with us before I die of shame. Dad's upset. You know you're the apple of his eye."

"I . . . I promised not to fuss about school . . . and now look at me!" Lisbeth burst out, feeling that she had erred unforgivably. "It isn't you—it's *me*," she continued, turning around to face her brother.

He was standing there looking so serious that she was startled. He was not teasing now at all. "Look, Lisbeth," he said, "everybody boils over once in a while. We'll take a walk later and feed the deer and you can tell me why you hate the idea of school. That won't be fussing. It'll be a secret."

"I'm ashamed to go down," she said. "I didn't mean to upset everything."'

"Don't be ashamed," her brother begged. "Let's you and I go down and see who blushes first."

"All right," Lisbeth agreed uncertainly. "But I don't know what to say."

"We'll just walk in and say we're sorry, and then we'll tie into the pudding." He took her hand. "Come on before you weaken."

When they entered the dining room, Robbie said, "Here come your contrite children. If we're good, may we sit down and eat our pudding?"

Lisbeth just looked first at Dad and then at Mother. She saw that their dessert was untouched. Then her brother poked her in the ribs.

"I didn't mean. . . ." she began.

"*We,*" Robbie whispered.

"We didn't mean to upset everything," she finished.

"Forget it," said Dad, taking up his spoon.

Mother had a sudden coughing fit. "Oh, dear," she gasped. "I swallowed the wrong way." When she recovered, she passed the cookies to Dad.

Then, looking out of the window, Lisbeth caught sight of Johnny the Buck walking out of the woods. "Look, Robbie. There's Johnny the Buck. Remember when the wolves chased him into the bay and you rowed out and got him?"

"He's changed more than you have," Robbie declared. "Look at those horns just showing in the velvet. Hurry up with your pudding. We'll go out and ask him if he remembers when he was a spike."

"Heaven forbid!" Dad exclaimed. "I'd hate to be asked to remember what I was like when I was a spike."

Lisbeth burst out laughing. "You were cute when you were a spike. I just know you were, Daddy."

CHAPTER 3

AFTER HER BURST of uncontrollable fury at the table that day in June, Lisbeth promised herself she would be on her guard and never give way like that again. She adored Robbie for helping her out of it so gracefully. Now that going to school appeared to be inevitable, she meant to carry it off without betraying that she was afraid. As the weeks passed, the packing season began and the cannery was humming and the fish dock piled high with salmon. Robbie was out on the boats and Dad was seldom in the house. Lisbeth felt the time sweeping past faster than it ever had before. She felt a tension growing within her, even though she tried not to think about going away.

One day near the end of August, Mother suggested that they go to the head of the bay to pick red huckleberries, because Robbie's boat was expected in and red huckleberry pie was his favorite. Mother got into her denim dress, and with pails and old Doggie Dash they rowed up the bay on the opposite side from home. There were scattered berry bushes in the Narrow Arm, but the only real patch where you could expect to fill a pail was near the head of the bay.

They climbed through the dense bushes on the steep hillside, singing as they picked. It was Mother's theory that if one sang lustily while in the huckleberry patch, any bears who chanced to be near would go away without disturbing the singer. They had to take turns singing, because the climbing was so difficult they got out of breath. When their pails were almost full and they had sung themselves out, Mother suggested they go elsewhere.

"This is an awful hillside, fit only for a monkey to climb about," she declared. "Let's row out to the island. Last year we found quite a few there. We should get enough to fill up our pails anyway."

"Oh, let's do!" Lisbeth cried. "It will be my last visit to the little island." She had not meant to say this. She hoped Mother would not guess that she meant her very last, because nothing would be the same afterwards.

The island stood offshore only a hundred yards or so. It was a little gem of an island, with a clam beach at one end and three or four spruce trees growing out of its crown.

As they started down to the boat, Mother said, "Lisbeth dear, you'll be back next summer. It isn't as if you were going away forever." She stopped talking as she crawled under a windfall; then she went on. "You've been so silent! Do let's talk about school. Sometimes I think we've waited too long, and that now it's more difficult than it would have been a year or two ago."

"Oh, no!" Lisbeth said quickly. "You haven't waited too long."

She followed Mother down to the skiff, climbing nimbly over the tumbled boulders with pail in hand. How could she talk about going to school? All she could think of was leaving Alaska. It was like going into exile or being banished. She couldn't imagine school except as a place where you were kept whether you liked it or not. She felt very strongly about it, but she couldn't talk about it. When they got to the skiff, she ordered the old dog into the bow while Mother took the berry pails to the stern. Then she pushed off and sat at the oars.

"You've got leaves in your hair like a wood nymph." Mother smiled as she tried to pin up the strands the brush had pulled loose from her own smooth braids. "Sometimes I think I should cut my hair like yours."

"Don't ever do it," Lisbeth protested. "I like it just as it is. Don't ever, ever change it." She looked directly into Mother's hazel-green eyes and went on earnestly. "I like everything exactly the way it is. I don't want anything to change—not ever!" She paused and glanced over her shoulder to see that she was coming into the island on the deep-water end, because the tide had begun to ebb.

"But everything *does* change, everything, including ourselves, whether we like it or not," Mother said gently. "I don't much like it myself. I used to hate to think of Robbie growing up. But look how foolish that was, Lisbeth. See what a fine young man he has become. Why, Robbie's more fun now than he ever was—and he understands so much!"

"He's different, just the same," Lisbeth said.

"Of course he's different," Mother agreed. "He'll

be nineteen next month. You'll be different, too, when you're nineteen. You'll be a young lady and you'll enjoy it just as much as Robbie's enjoying being a young man." Before Lisbeth could protest, she went on. "Going out to school will prepare you for growing up."

"It's bad enough without wasting time being prepared," Lisbeth said uncomfortably. "It happens anyway—no matter what you do."

They were alongside the steep end of the island now, and she deftly shipped oars and reached out to catch hold of the roughly seamed rocks.

"There's just a chance—a slim one, I know, but a chance nevertheless—that you might like the preparation," Mother said cautiously.

Lisbeth jumped out on the rocks and held the boat while Mother climbed up. The old dog was already sniffing around above them, where grass and tiny seedling spruce trees grew out of the crevices. When she had made the boat fast, Lisbeth looked pleadingly at Mother. "Don't let's talk about it," she begged.

"You make Dad and me feel so awful," Mother protested, "like the wicked stepmother in the fairy tales."

For a while Lisbeth said nothing as they made

their way along the steep rocks toward the other end of the island. She had not thought how Mother and Dad might feel about doing what they thought they ought to do. "You aren't a wicked stepmother," she said finally. Then, as they reached the shell-strewn beach, she admitted that she didn't know how to talk about school. She said this a little stiffly, trying not to seem ignorant.

"I'll tell you what I think it will be like," Mother said, seeming not to notice her discomfiture. "The bishop will have his office there, because it's a church school, and a headmistress and teachers for all the different subjects will live there. There'll be girls from all parts of the United States and maybe some from Canada or South America—country girls and city girls."

They were in the brush now, hunting out the huckleberry bushes. Mother's voice sounded gay and promising. "You'll have a nice room and a room-mate. The booklet says that each new girl has an old girl for a roommate during the first semester. She helps you get acquainted and helps you learn the school routine."

"What if I don't like her?" Lisbeth demurred. She had found a good bush and perched herself on the top of an old stump to pick. "This bush is simply hanging with berries, simply red with them," she added irrelevantly.

"I've got a good one, too." Mother's voice came from the high bushes a little distance away. "I suppose if you don't like her you'll have to put up with her as politely as possible, until the end of the semester."

"I don't expect I'll like her," Lisbeth commented.

"Oh, darling!" Mother despaired. "I'm afraid you're making it more difficult than need be. You may like your roommate very much indeed. And if you do, it would be fun to ask her to come and visit you next summer. Wouldn't it?"

"But, *Mother!*" Lisbeth wailed. "What would I do with a . . . with a girl in toeless shoes in a place like this? I don't want anyone snooping into all my special spots, scaring the animals and . . . and everything."

"It was just an idea," Mother said faintly. After a pause her voice went on more bravely. "I know one part of it you're bound to like."

"Coming home for Christmas," Lisbeth guessed. She had filled her pail and now sat on her mossy stump eating the tart red berries that were left on the bush.

Mother broke through the bushes, laughing, and

came toward her. "What an imp you are! No. I meant seeing Uncle Jim in San Francisco. I want to see him myself."

"Yes," Lisbeth agreed thoughtfully. "I'll love seeing Uncle Jim." She stopped and sighed. "But I don't think I need to go to school just to see him on the way. I just can't like it, Mother. But don't worry. I expect I'll live through it."

"I'm not so sure Dad and I will," Mother replied. "We must write often, dear, and tell each other how we are getting on." She leaned upon the stump where Lisbeth was sitting. "Whenever you get lonesome, you'll know we are missing you like everything."

For a moment they were silent, listening to the soft shush of the breeze in the spruce trees above them. Dash watched them from his bed in the moss, as though divining that they were about to start home. Impulsively Lisbeth threw her arms around Mother's neck and kissed her. "I'll remember everything you've said," she promised fervently. "Everything."

She slid down from the stump and led the way back to the beach on a narrow mink trail she had discovered coming up. When they got back to the boat, they put Dash in the stern and sat together on

the rowing seat, one at each oar. They started homeward with the ebbing tide and a fair breeze from
the mountains. *"Pull* away! *Pull* away!" They
chanted, until their rhythm was smooth and the
skiff was gliding homeward over the rippling water.

It was their last day away from home together
that summer. A few days later they began getting
ready for the trip south.

"You'll need everything new," Mother said.
"Thank goodness, I can let down the hem of your
pleated skirt. You can wear one of your silk shirts
and a sweater with that on the plane."

"Shall I have to wear dress-up clothes all the time
—every day till I come home?" Lisbeth asked.

"Your clothes will be very simple," Mother explained. "Skirts and sweaters or simple dresses for
school, a dress and coat for going out, and something
suitable for dinner and the school parties. You'll
be comfortable in them. The booklet suggests that
you take clothes for skiing on week ends. Shall I
put in the ones you have or would you rather have
new ones?"

"I'd rather take the ones I have," Lisbeth answered. "But I can't ski! Shall I *have* to ski?"

Mother fished around in the garment bag for
Lisbeth's ski pants. "You may take lessons if you

want to. You can learn to do all kinds of things, you know. Remember when we first thought of your going away we went over all the things, like music and dancing and everything you might like to do?"

It was all these things that Lisbeth dreaded, but she did not say so. She was not afraid of the books. She knew how to study if she made herself do it. What troubled her was her vision of other girls skimming down mountains on skis, while she stood awkwardly on the side lines. She was sure she could outlast any of them on snowshoes, but she would never have a chance to show it. She had a vague contempt for sports. They seemed pointless and silly to her. She rowed well and could climb mountains with skill and intelligence, and she could read charts and steer a boat, because these things were all a part of her daily life. To be skillful in order to beat someone else seemed to her to be merely a rather unpleasant way of showing off. Suppose someone *was* tennis champion! Suppose some school *did* beat another at football! What of it? She had heard the sports announcers on the radio yelling like crazy men about a football game, and she wondered how they could even pretend to believe it was so exciting or important. As Long Paul said, outsiders were always trying to get the best of one another. To Lisbeth this business of always trying to win seemed mean and unworthy. The voices on the radio often seemed to come from a fearful and disgusting world that she dreaded to enter.

"I think I'd like dancing," she said at last, trying not to seem afraid. "If they don't have contests."

"I don't believe this school goes in much for contests or competitions," Mother answered. "But you will be encouraged to have interests outside your schoolwork." She examined the ski pants and laid them on the bed. "Of course, some of the girls will have attitudes different from ours. Some of them will probably have a great many clothes, but I don't think that's necessary. We'll get you enough pretty dresses."

Lisbeth felt herself growing more and more uncomfortable. She wandered away from the house, where the preparations made everything bleak. A little way beyond the house she found Faithful Sue lying in the grass, chewing her cud. Beside her was her little spotted fawn, Susanna. Nearby, Billy the Third was nibbling fastidiously at the tips of a blueberry bush. Lisbeth spoke to Sue quietly, as she approached and sat down in the moss near her. With a flick of his tail, Billy turned away from his blueberry bush and came to have his head rubbed.

"I've come to say good-by," Lisbeth told them. "I might not see you again and I shall be gone for a long, long time."

The doe continued chewing her cud as she gazed at her, and Lisbeth looked long into the great dark eyes before she went on. "You must be careful this winter, Sue. Stay close by the house all the time with Susanna. You mustn't let the wolves get you. You must be here when I come home." She put her arm around Billy and let her head lean against his neck. Feeling sad and already lonely beyond words, she got to her feet. But she could not take her hand away from Billy's little dome of a head. She could feel the bumps where his horns were going to be. Billy would be a spike next summer.

Johnny the Buck had been away for several days, probably off in the woods somewhere, scratching the velvet off his horns. They were all getting ready for autumn, which was their time to prepare for winter. Now, at the end of August, everything was beginning to change again. But the biggest change of all was hers, for tomorrow or next day the plane would come from Juneau and then, in only a minute or two, Hermit Bay would be out of her sight.

That evening the *Vega* came in to unload fish. After supper Lisbeth went down to the wharf to say good-by to Long Paul and Ole. The cannery was humming, running overtime to get the fish in the cans. But the crew of the *Vega* were at leisure. Their work was done and their boat washed down, ready to go out to the fishing grounds again in the morning. Lisbeth climbed over the stringer and down the ladder, leaving Dash, with his red tongue out, watching anxiously from above. She went along the deck to the galley and there she found her friends, silently drinking coffee.

"Look out, Paul!" Ole warned as she stepped over the sea guard. "Har come the boss." He sprang to his feet and dusted the already shining bench with his big red bandanna. In a flash he had a bottle of root beer and a glass in front of her.

"You come just in time," Paul told her. "We need advice."

"How you t'ink we look in red cap wit' long beak like ski fellers wear, wit' goggles underneat'?" Ole asked with appropriate gestures.

"Funny!" Lisbeth laughed. "I think you'd look funny. Why?"

"Good," Ole said. "No red caps for us."

Long Paul took his pipe out of his mouth and

held it in his hand. "Yesterday we see a feller wearing this thing on his head," he explained to Lisbeth. "A fisherman he was. Goggles and all."

"A commercial fisherman?" Lisbeth asked incredulously.

"Ya. We buy fish from him," Long Paul replied.

For a moment all three were silent, contemplating this extraordinary vision. Finally Lisbeth said, "He must have been an outsider."

The men agreed, and for a while they talked about how things were changing, with more boats from the outside coming to the Straits every year.

"Things are changing for me, too," Lisbeth told them. "Tomorrow or next day Mother's taking me south to school—clear to California."

The importance of her announcement was reflected in the long pause that followed. Then Paul and Ole made jokes about how it was a good thing she was going to school, because she could come back and give Ole lessons. Long Paul declared that he himself was too old to learn. But the jokes soon wore thin and there was another pause.

"It will be good to see something of the world," Paul said, looking at her. "You will do good if you keep your eyes open. If a storm comes up, take to a harbor until it passes."

"And don't run on no rocks," Ole put in. "If there ain't no harbor, take to the deep water and ride her out."

"People outside is different," Long Paul went on between pulls on his pipe. "They got ideas like we do not. First thing you do, you chart that school and all the people—every last one of 'em. Then set your course an' steer right through. Don't let nobody else steer for you."

"Oh, thank you, Paul. I'll remember everything you've said. I'll run at slow speed till I've got the whole thing charted." Lisbeth glowed with confidence. She had hold of something now. She would chart the layout. Then she would know where she was going.

C H A P T E R   4

THE NEXT MORNING the two light traveling bags
were closed and locked. By nine-thirty Lisbeth,
watching the fog thin overhead, gave up her last
hope that a thick spell might set in and keep the
plane from coming down in the bay. She stood staring disconsolately out of the window, dressed in her
jeans and an old sweater, which she had kept on in
the hope that something would delay the plane.

Mother was trying to be cheerful. "Robbie will
be leaving here in about a week," she said. "He may
reach San Francisco while we are still there."

"It will be good to have him in the same state, anyway," Lisbeth remarked. In the next breath she cried, "Here comes Dad as fast as he can walk."

"You'd better run up and dress," Mother told her. "He's probably heard from Juneau."

"I want to wait. Please let me," Lisbeth begged. "I can change in a couple of minutes if the plane's coming."

Mother said, "All right, dear," and came and stood behind her to watch Dad hurrying along the walk. When he reached the porch, Lisbeth hung back while he opened the door.

"Everybody ready?" Dad asked. "The plane's on its way." He looked at his daughter. "You're not going in those duds, are you?" He picked her up and hugged her and put her on her feet again. "Scurry," he ordered. "If we do this real fast, it won't be nearly as bad as pulling a tooth."

Lisbeth ran into the hall and up the stairs without stopping. Her clothes were lying on the bed, ready to put on. It did not take her long to change into the blouse and sweater and plaid skirt. Then she stood with the little green felt hat in her hands, looking around her room. She had taken no interest in the packing, but now there were ever so many things she wanted to take with her. She thrust her arms into her topcoat and hunched it on. Then she went to her dresser and swept a brown bear's tooth, a pair of eagle's talons, and a miniature yellow cedar totem pole into her hat. She picked up the green, pear-shaped lucky stone an old Indian woman had given her when she was little. She held it in her hand, feeling its smooth, cool surface before she dropped it into the hat with her other treasures. Finally, she closed the folding frame that held the pictures of Mother and Dad and slipped it into the pocket of her coat.

"Hurry, dear," Mother called anxiously. "It will take a while to get down to the wharf. We don't want to rush."

Suddenly Lisbeth did want to rush. Suddenly she wanted to get the departure over with. She ran down the stairs with her coat askew and her hat in her hand. Dash jumped up from his place at the foot of the stairs and trotted into the living room after her.

"Mother, I've got some things to put in my bag," she panted. "I just thought of them."

Mother opened her purse and fished around in it to find the keys. Lisbeth waited what seemed to be minutes on end until the bag was opened. Then she knelt down and found places for her keepsakes.

When she had them all tucked away, Mother said, "Let me straighten your coat while Dad locks the bag." She straightened the collar of the coat and pulled down the sleeves. "Better put your hat on," she suggested. "Have you got your gloves?"

Lisbeth darted for the stairs, pulling the hat down hard on the back of her head. "I forgot them!" she cried, clattering up to her room again.

"Take it easy," Dad called after her. "You'll blow a gasket if you don't look out."

Lisbeth dashed back to the living room, gloves in hand, and flung open the door. "Hush," she whispered as she stood listening. "I thought I heard it."

"It hasn't quite had time," Dad told her. "But you can begin listening. You've got the sharpest ears."

Lisbeth crossed the porch and descended the steps, with the fingers of one hand touching the top of Doggie Dash's head. I won't look back, she thought, as she walked down the flat stones leading to the boardwalk. This is the worst part of it. She almost groaned with the ache in her heart, not daring to glance at the cedar house there behind her. Tears were smarting in her eyes and she blinked them back, determined that she would not cry.

Then Billy the deer butted his head into her from

behind and she stumbled. Furiously she turned upon him. "It's just like you to turn up when you're not wanted," she cried. Then she saw that Faithful Sue and little spotted Susanna were standing on the rise in front of the house, looking after her with their long ears pointed forward. Lisbeth's lower lip began to tremble and she pursed her mouth to try to stop it.

Dad dropped the bags and came quickly forward. "Billy," he said, " this is bad enough without you." His voice was so tight that Lisbeth suspected he wished he could throw the luggage into the bay and go back to the house and stay there. He gave Billy a slap on the rump and sent him bounding up the slope to Sue. Looking at Lisbeth, he said helplessly, "There now!"

Knowing that he wanted to comfort her, she nodded her head vigorously, because she could not speak. Slowly she proceeded along the walk, listening, longing to hear the plane before they reached Dad's office and had to stop there and wait. She knew how the three deer looked behind her there, standing on the rise in front of the house, watching her go forever. When I come back, I'll smell different to them, she thought. My voice will sound different. It will be a different me coming back.

Behind her, Mother and Dad were silent and their footsteps were slow. When they reached the cannery store, Dad put the bags inside the door. "Come on in," he said. "We can wait here in the office. It won't be for long, if he's going to get you to Juneau in time to make connections with the Seattle plane."

"I'll go up and watch out of the storeroom window," said Lisbeth, heading for the stairs.

"All right," Dad assented. "Sing out when you sight him."

In the upstairs window Lisbeth and Doggie Dash waited for the plane. She sat on an empty crate and leaned on the sill of the open window. Looking toward the Straits, she could see only mountains, the long shoulder of one of them forming the point that sheltered the bay. Heavyhearted, she sat and watched. It was over this shoulder the plane would come. The fog was gone now except for a few streamers lying in the canyons of the mountains. The low hum of machinery in the cannery filled the air, and she listened intently to catch the drone of the approaching plane. She listened with such concentration that she could not think. She did not want to notice anything. She couldn't bear to say good-by to Hermit Bay. The hum of the cannery machinery lulled her, but she knew that the moment the drone of the plane was added to it she would recognize it.

When she heard it, she did not wait to sight the plane but rushed down the stairs, shouting, "I hear it! It's coming!"

Dad went to the door and stood listening. "Sure it isn't just the cannery you hear?" he asked.

Watching his face, Lisbeth said, "Listen again." Then she saw that he heard the plane's drone.

"It puzzles me," he said, picking up the bags, "how anyone with such small ears as yours can hear so well. Come on, Mother," he added.

Before they had reached the cannery buildings, the little plane came swiftly over the shoulder of the mountain and glided down to the water. When they came out on the wharf, it was taxiing in to the float on its big pontoons. Lisbeth's heart quickened as Dad ran down the slip and dropped the bags, in order to catch the wing of the plane. With the engine silent, she could hear the noise of machinery and the shouts of men on the fish dock. Everyone was working and the wharf was deserted. She followed Mother down to the float with Doggie Dash beside her.

The young pilot jumped down and stood by the open door of the plane. He answered Dad's greeting and told him the flying was clear all the way in, and that they should make their connection on the dot.

Then Dad kissed Mother and helped her into the little cabin. Lisbeth sank down and threw her arms around Doggie Dash. "Take it easy, old fellow, while I'm gone," she whispered to him.

Dad picked her up and hugged her. "Be brave, honey," he said in her ear, "and don't let them scuttle you!"

For a moment she clung to him, then she let him boost her into the plane. Dash started after her, and Dad pulled him back and held him by the collar. The little door closed, and she pressed her face against the window to watch them. The engine began roaring. The white water flew thicker and faster, and the float and Dad and Dash were out of sight. The plane turned into the wind and the roaring increased. Lisbeth watched the pontoon on her side leave the water. The mountains circled tipsily around them, and then she saw the cannery and Dad and Doggie Dash, standing where they had left them on the float. Dad waved his hat and held it in the air as long as she could see him.

Lisbeth set her jaws, not daring to look at Mother. Staring wide-eyed out of the little window, she watched the magnificent peaks of the mountain and the blue water making thin white scallops at their feet. Then Hermit Bay was gone.

She sat rigid and miserable, staring down at the white-capped water of the strait, listening to the roaring drone of the engine. After a while she felt her muscles relax, and looked around to find Mother smiling at her. The departure was over. They were on their way, and all too soon she saw the buildings of Juneau below them, clinging to the hillside and stretching along the beach for room in this perpendicular country.

Mother, who was quite good at taking off in a plane, hated coming down. She reached over and took Lisbeth's hand as they began to lose altitude. Lisbeth loved coming down best of all. She had Mother's hand firmly in her lap while she looked down, waiting for the pontoon to skip against the water—skip—skip—and then the white spray flying. In the excitement she forgot for a moment that she was not going back. Then from the plane landing a taxi took them directly to the airport where the big Seattle plane was loading.

That evening Lisbeth ate dinner in their hotel room in Seattle. The next day in the early afternoon she stepped off an air liner onto the ground of the San Francisco airport. Her first impression was of dryness and blank space, upon which triangular shapes and arcs and straight lines were superimposed in the glaring sunlight. Huge planes roared confidently on the runways, where no people were seen. The people moving about the buildings, even the stream of passengers among whom she moved, seemed insignificant. Through the gate they went and into a blank-walled room, where a harsh mechanical voice seemed to rend her ears, and the voices and laughter of the passengers was mere chattering. It was oppressive and frightening. She felt that they dared not stop. They must keep moving, keep moving with the stream. Her ears were ringing and she felt uncomfortable and panicky.

Then Uncle Jim appeared. He emerged out of the crowd as a bear emerges out of the woods. She had not seen him coming and then he was before them, his hat in his hand, his red hair like a torch in that impersonal room. He gave Mother a hug, upsetting her hat, while people hurried past them on either side. Then he turned to Lisbeth and put an arm around her shoulder. "How's my baby?" he said, and it seemed that instead of two years it had been only a little while ago that she had last seen him. He had always called her "baby," and he was the only person she would have permitted to do so.

Now that they had Uncle Jim, everything worked like magic. He got their bags, guided them to his car, and insisted that they both sit in the front seat with him. Lisbeth's fears dwindled away, and even when they were going lickety-split along the crowded highway to the city, Uncle Jim made it seem quite safe and sane. He seemed so perfectly at home, so undisturbed, asking them questions about Dad and the cannery, as though the stream of cars on the road meant nothing to him. Uncle Jim had made his money in Alaska, and now he lived in San Francisco when he was not in New York, which seemed as far away as London to Lisbeth. There was no doubt that Uncle Jim was a city man now, but Lisbeth felt that it had not hurt him. He was just the same inside. She knew that years ago Uncle Jim's heart had been broken by love, but she didn't know just how, because she could not remember all that had been said then. But that was why he was a bachelor and had no children of his own.

As they reeled along the curving road past bare brown hills and row upon row of white houses, Lisbeth felt the hardness of the glaring light. It's because there are no trees, she thought, no forest to soften the light. Now the city lay all around them, a city of boxes, of angles and cubes and towers. It all seemed hard, not with the living hardness of rock but with an impersonal and artificial hardness that Lisbeth could only feel and could not define. Soon they were surrounded by streetcars, buses, automobiles, and thousands of people, surging this way and then that way with the traffic lights. Involuntarily Lisbeth shrank back, as if to escape from the harshness of the noise and the smell of burned gasoline in the air.

Uncle Jim reached over and patted her hand. "Isn't it great, baby?" he asked. "This is Market Street."

Lisbeth was so taken aback she said nothing for a moment. But she looked anew at the crowded street and felt the surge of traffic as the light changed and they moved forward again.

"It *is* exciting," she admitted, "but I'm glad you're with us."

They turned off the street and rounded a block and came back to it again. Lisbeth felt that the maze of buildings they were in was far more confusing and dangerous than the ridged forest of Hermit Bay. Then they shot up a hill so fast that Mother gave a little gasp, and Lisbeth felt as though she were being held forcibly against the back of the seat.

They bounced over the top, crossed the street just as the light changed, and rolled smoothly into the driveway of a handsome building. Lisbeth caught glimpses of small clipped trees across the street, as Uncle Jim pulled up in front of the entrance.

A uniformed doorman immediately opened the car door, and a porter came running out to get their bags. "I'll park the car," Uncle Jim told them. "I'll be right back. You go on up."

He drove off swiftly, leaving Lisbeth staring anxiously after him. She had a quick impression of patches of bright green lawn bordered with yellow and blue flowers, of sun on the white facade of the building, and of the rather awesome doorman waiting for them to go in. She slipped past him and followed Mother into the stately lobby of the hotel.

She stood looking around while Mother was at the desk. There was no rush in here. It was quiet and the light was soft. From somewhere music drifted in. A few people sat in the deep chairs, talking softly or listening to the music. Lisbeth looked at the high arched windows with their long rich drapes, at the marble steps leading away at one side, and at the thick red carpet. She would have liked to bury her face in the flowers that stood on dark gleaming tables. This hotel was different from anything she had seen before. She lifted her head and delicately sniffed the air.

Then she became aware of a girl only a year or two older than herself, walking with two sleekly dressed women toward the doors. The girl wore a gray squirrel coat and thin stockings. She passed quite close, staring at Lisbeth with insolent, amused eyes. For the first time Lisbeth became aware of her old plaid skirt and her coat with the sleeves that were too short. For the first time in her life she felt uncouth. Somehow, she could not tell how, her dignity was shaken. She turned away from that insolent stare, feeling the color burning in her face, as she made herself walk slowly to Mother's side.

"We can go up now," Mother said, and they followed in the wake of the porter carrying their bags.

In their room, Lisbeth's eyes fell first upon a long mirror in one of the doors. While Mother stood in the window exclaiming over the view, Lisbeth regarded her reflection in the mirror. It was the first time she had ever looked critically at herself. Her standard of comparison was the girl she had just seen in the lobby. She saw herself as that sleek red-lipped girl must have seen her, and all her resentment against the outside world flared up anew. At home she had not given a thought to how she looked, but here she seemed to be growing out of her clothes, as though she were too big and outlandishly robust. She was scowling fiercely at the redhead in the mirror when Uncle Jim's knock came at the door. She pulled off the absurd green hat that made her look as though she had too much hair, and threw it on the bed. When Mother opened the door and greeted Uncle Jim, she had the offending coat off and was scrutinizing her costume of skirt, sweater, and bobby socks. I look like a ten-year-old, she thought miserably.

"Jim, the room is lovely," Mother exclaimed. "You were sweet to have flowers here for us. Come in and sit down. I'll order tea."

"Thank you, Flossie. Don't order for me, though. I'm going to leave you to rest a while. I'll be around to pick you up for dinner and the show. I've got tickets for a musical that's straight from Broadway."

"Oh, Uncle Jim," Lisbeth cried, "I can't go. I haven't got any clothes yet. I look awful—I know I do!"

"Nobody will notice, dear," Mother said, surprised at the outburst. "Tomorrow we'll start shopping and get everything you need."

"Mother, I just can't do it!" Lisbeth declared.

"People will stare! Please. You go with Uncle Jim. I'll stay right here in this room."

"Why, baby, do you really think I'd let you do that?" Uncle Jim crossed the room and took her two hands. He stepped back and looked at her. "You're a honey," he declared. "You're going to be the prettiest girl in San Francisco by dinnertime. Come on!" He started for the door. "Flossie, you have your tea and a rest. We'll be back for you about six o'clock. Early dinner on account of the show."

"Jim Millar, what are you going to do?" Mother demanded.

"We're going shopping," he stated. "Don't look so horrified. I know a young lady in one of our best shops. She has impeccable taste. Lisbeth will be turned out in just the right clothes for thirteen-going-on-fourteen. I swear, Flossie, you will be delighted when you see her." Uncle Jim looked very earnest indeed.

Mother burst out laughing. She put her arm around Lisbeth's shoulders and gave her a gentle push. "Go ahead, dear," she said. "You two will have fun, no matter what you buy. It's already late. You haven't much time."

Lisbeth half ran down the hall to keep up with Uncle Jim's long strides. In no time they were in a taxi, making a breath-taking lunge down the hill. Then they were in the traffic, creeping along past shops and people, crowds of people, while Uncle Jim explained the efficiency of the taxicab in a large city. Lisbeth sat on the edge of the seat, watching the people gather at the crossings and surge across at the signal. She was apprehensive lest something go wrong, and the buses, streetcars, and automobiles get out of hand and send the people helter-skelter in all directions. She had thought it was crowded at the airport, but that had been nothing compared to this. But being out with Uncle Jim was like visiting a terrifying other world with one's guardian angel. It was exciting but not panicky. They passed stores and small shops with elaborate window displays, and street corners where flower vendors stood selling their wares. Lisbeth cried, "Oh look," so surprised was she to see the masses of flowers right out in the open, amidst all that confusion. The taxi slid up to the sidewalk in front of a blue glass door, over which a blue glass marquee reached out to the curb.

"Climb out, baby," said Uncle Jim as Lisbeth hesitated. She got out on the sidewalk cautiously, and stood so close to her uncle that he bumped her with his elbow when he reached in his pocket for change for the driver.

Ahead of them, a woman was entering the shop. The door opened and she went in. As it started to close, Lisbeth hurried forward to catch it. But it sprang back before her outstretched hand, and she found herself rushing headlong into the shop.

Uncle Jim came after her. "It's got an electric eye that makes it work," he explained. "I should have warned you."

"It makes you feel as if someone had played a practical joke on you," Lisbeth commented, not daring to look at the few women on the main floor of the shop.

"It's a trap," Uncle Jim sympathized. "The first time I ever encountered one I was in a hurry and lunged for the door and nearly fell into the shop when it opened like that."

"You did?" Lisbeth looked at him. She could not imagine Uncle Jim ever being surprised at anything. Her embarrassment left her as they passed through the scented air of the perfume section and entered a gold-and-green elevator. She was excited and apprehensive when the door slid back. This time she stayed close to her uncle's side, as they stepped out.

A lady in black, with gleaming pearls, seemed to float forward over the deep carpet to meet them.

"May we see Miss Trevor, please?" said Uncle Jim. The lady murmured, and drifted away.

In a moment a young woman with sparkling brown eyes came quickly toward them from a large room beyond. She smiled at Lisbeth and at Uncle Jim. "How do you do, Mr. Millar? May I help you?" she said.

"Thank you. We need a great deal of help," Uncle Jim replied. "Miss Trevor, this is my niece, Lisbeth Craig. She left Hermit Bay, Alaska, yesterday morning. We need a whole outfit from shoes to hat by dinnertime. I hope you won't mind our being so late."

Miss Trevor said, "Of course not," and asked Lisbeth questions about Alaska as she led her to a fitting room. Then she began talking about clothes as though clothes were the most important things in the world.

When Miss Trevor had finished with her, Lisbeth walked out of the shop glancing into every mirror she passed. She was immensely curious about the fact that she could have changed so. Her new underwear felt smooth against her skin. She liked the dark-blue dress with its white collar and tie, and the blue coat with a cape around the shoulders. Even the little hat with a feather on one side was comfortable. She did not look at all like the girl in the squirrel coat, nor did she look like the reflection she had seen in the mirror in their hotel room. She felt different, too. She could not say just how, and when Uncle Jim asked her she hesitated before she answered.

Finally she said, "It's as if you had worked a spell on me that changed me into somebody else—somebody sort of related to me but not exactly me."

"Heaven forbid!" Uncle Jim muttered, as they stood on the curb looking for a cab. The streets were more crowded than ever now. "Taxi! Taxi!" shouted Uncle Jim, waving one arm wildly at a cruising cab as he held onto Lisbeth with the other.

C H A P T E R　　　　　5

DURING THEIR SIX DAYS in San Francisco, Uncle Jim
introduced Lisbeth to a part of the outside world of
which she knew nothing except that it existed. He
persuaded Mother, somewhat against her will, that
this was the best preparation Lisbeth could have before going to school. "Just so she'll know what
they're talking about," he argued. He took them to
the theater, a symphony concert, the opening night
of the opera. They visited museums, art galleries,
and the park conservatory. He and Lisbeth saw the
aquarium and the zoo, and they drove across the bay

to see Robbie's college. Shopping took up the mornings.

When Mother tried to tell Uncle Jim that Lisbeth should stay in for a day to rest, he merely replied that he didn't want the girls at school to have anything on his baby, and off they went again.

So much was happening that at times Lisbeth forgot entirely that she was on her way to school. Bewildered and enchanted by turns, she felt like an expanding bubble, full of color and reflections, but about to pop any minute. This was a world of which she had never dreamed. It was like living in a storybook. The people whom she had so dreaded to live among were merely part of the background. By the end of the week she began to feel as though she had spent a large part of her life in San Francisco. Even a letter from Dad failed to bring Alaska closer. It stirred a sadness in her, like the memory of having been hurt when one has forgotten the cause of the hurt, but it brought Hermit Bay no closer. She was dazzled by a flood of new impressions.

To Lisbeth it seemed very sudden when, on their sixth day, Mother closed and locked her new trunk and the hotel porter came and took it away.

"I think I enjoyed buying your clothes more than you did," said Mother.

But Lisbeth's mind was following her trunk. "I don't expect it will be as nice there as it is here," she said apprehensively.

"Oh, it's nicer. Much nicer," Mother replied. "It's got lots of flowers and trees. Just wait. You'll see!"

In the middle of the week Mother had made a trip down to the school to talk with the headmistress. It was on the day when Uncle Jim and Lisbeth went to the zoo in the morning and a matinee in the afternoon, because he said it was a good thing to sit down after you had tramped around the zoo all morning. Mother had come back on the evening train very much pleased with what she had seen. Now, with the trunk gone, Lisbeth's old feeling of apprehension returned and she did not want to talk about school.

Late that afternoon, as they were getting ready to dress for dinner, the telephone bell rang. Lisbeth, expecting to hear Uncle Jim's voice, picked up the instrument and said, "Hello, Uncle Jim."

"This isn't Uncle Jim, little wild girl," the voice replied.

"Why, Robbie! Are you downstairs? Where are you?"

"I'm across the bay. . . ."

"Come over quick, Robbie. I have to go away in the morning. You got here just in time."

"I'll be there in thirty minutes," Robbie said. "Wait for me." The telephone clicked and Lisbeth knew he had hung up. She turned to Mother. "He hung up before I could ask him anything," she said. "But he'll be here in thirty minutes."

"I'm glad he's here for our last evening." Mother beamed.

"He called me wild girl again." Lisbeth chuckled. "Just wait until he sees me! He won't know me."

She brushed her short hair back from her face and upwards at the nape of her neck. Uncle Jim was taking them to a very special place for dinner, because it was their last night. Mother was wearing her new suit and Lisbeth put on the blue-and-white-checked taffeta they had bought for her to wear to dinner at school.

Uncle Jim arrived first, and immediately telephoned the restaurant that they would be late and that there would be four of them instead of three. Then he fished in his coat pocket and brought out a small box wrapped in white paper. "Here, baby," he said, handing it to Lisbeth. "Put this in your suitcase and don't open it until you go to bed tomorrow night." As she took the little box, he went on. "I'm going East tomorrow, myself. This is a little good-by present."

She looked at him gravely. "Thank you, Uncle Jim. Thank you for everything." It came over her that Uncle Jim, also, was going to be alone. It was a bond between them. She put the little box in her suitcase and hunted around until she found her lucky stone. She put it in Uncle Jim's hand. "This is awfully lucky," she told him gravely. "Keep it with you all the time."

Then she went on quickly. "I'm going to surprise Robbie right out of his wits. May I wait for him downstairs, Mother? I want to see if he'll know me."

"Certainly, dear," Mother assented. "But be sure to take the right elevator."

"Don't worry about her," said Uncle Jim, still holding the little stone and rubbing it with his thumb. "She could go downtown alone and get back all by herself now."

It was Lisbeth's first venture out of the room alone. Before her the red carpet stretched down the long corridor. She passed one bank of elevators and kept on to the next, which would take her to the main lobby. It was a busy hour and the elevator was full of people. She pulled in her elbows and tried not to touch any of them, while she stared at the door, feeling self-conscious and on the verge of panic. She had forgotten that the lobby was so crowded at this hour. But she could not retreat now. When the elevator door slid back, she moved out with the rest of the people. For a moment she hesitated; then she thrust out her chin and walked to a chair in front of the main entrance.

She sat in the high-backed chair, watching people come in and go out. Through the glass she could catch glimpses of cars and taxis and swerving headlights. Women came through the doors in sweeping skirts and furs and orchids, looking like pictures, but the men in their uniformly dark suits seemed dull and, Lisbeth thought, old. How everyone would stare if big handsome Ole were to come in, wearing his plaid shirt and blue jeans. When Robbie did not come immediately, she began to grow nervous, fearing he might have used some other entrance. She sat with her hands clasped tightly in her lap, her eyes on the doors, forgetting now that she wanted to surprise him, wanting only to see him.

Finally the doors swung back farther than anyone else had pushed them, and there was Robbie already three strides on his way to the elevator. Lisbeth sprang out of the chair and ran after him, barely avoiding a collision with the passing people.

"Robbie!" she cried in a loud whisper, as she caught hold of his sleeve. He was hatless and dressed in a dark suit and topcoat that made his hair seem blonder than ever.

He stopped in his tracks and looked down at her. She saw his astonishment, then the recognition in his eyes, and she knew he was fooling when he said, "Excuse me. I'm sure I know you—but I don't quite place you."

Lisbeth clung to his arm and laughed. "I thought I might have missed you," she said. "I *do* look different, don't I?"

"Why, it's my little wild girl!" he exclaimed. "Where's that mop of hair? Where are those jeans? Stand back so I can see you!"

People looked at them and smiled, as Lisbeth, oblivious of their glances, stepped back and stood gazing triumphantly at her brother.

He looked at her admiringly for a moment, then took her arm. "I'm struck dumb," he told her. "Honestly, Lisbeth, I never thought you'd survive it. I thought I'd find you in the monkey cage at the zoo. And look at you!"

Secure at her brother's side, she was no longer so acutely aware of the people. Then she forgot them altogether and laughed with Robbie, as they waited for the elevator and ascended to the long corridor. She even forgot about tomorrow, so pleased was she with Robbie's admiration. She felt quite grown-up and confident.

That night at dinner, Uncle Jim and Robbie were in such high spirits that Mother had to beg them to stop making her laugh, so that she could eat. They were at Uncle Jim's favorite restaurant, where their table was in an alcove of windows and there were real candles. They looked down upon the myriad lights encircling the bay, and the soft orange lights spanning the velvet-black water where the bridges crossed. There was a romantic atmosphere about the little restaurant that made Lisbeth feel one must be very special indeed to be there at all.

Afterwards, they drove to the top of the hill in Uncle Jim's car. The wind had died away and the September night was warm. They got out of the car and stood in a row at the concrete balustrade, to look again at the lights of the city and the bay.

Uncle Jim put his arm around Lisbeth's shoulders. "There won't be any time for last words tomorrow," he said. "We'll all be off in opposite directions. What a lot we'll have to say to each other when we meet again."

Uneasily Lisbeth realized that once more everything was changing. She could think of nothing to say.

Mother filled in the pause. "You've been awfully good to us, Jim," she said. "We've seen and heard enough to keep us in pleasant memories for a long time."

Lisbeth found her voice. "Oh, yes, Uncle Jim. We couldn't have got on without you. You make everything so exciting! I wish you could come to school with me."

Robbie burst out laughing. "Make him go with you, Sister. Our elders ought to be given a term in school every now and then, to make them realize what we're up against."

"Why, Robert!" said Mother, in a shocked voice. "When you talk like that, you make it sound like a . . . a term in jail. And it's no such thing. School days are the most delightful days of our lives."

"Why, *Mother,*" Robbie teased, "how can you tell such fibs?"

"Never mind," Uncle Jim counseled. "When I am tottering around with a cane, you two will be talking about your school days as if they were a beautiful dream."

"Why does it take so long to make them into a dream?" Lisbeth asked.

"Who's going to answer that one?" Robbie challenged them.

"I am," said Mother promptly. "It takes so long because most of us are not perceptive enough to know when our lives are good. But I think Lisbeth is. She won't have to wait until Uncle Jim totters."

"Bravo!" said Uncle Jim, and with that last word they all got back into his car.

Lisbeth was beginning to learn one thing about changes. When they were actually happening, you did not have much time to think about them. She and Mother got on the train at eight o'clock the next morning. It was her first trip by rail and everything was new. She had a sort of empty feeling, because she knew this was the last lap of her journey to school, but the feeling was submerged in the excitement of eating in the dining car while the landscape rushed past. Later, in her seat, she watched the towns and orchards slide swiftly past her window. Banks of vivid flowers flashed by, and her imagination seized upon them to counteract the loneliness of the distant barren hills and the interminable monotony of white stucco houses. It seemed so strange—this land without forests and high mountains to shade the glare of the sky, a land where trees at the roadsides looked dry and brittle, and the hills in the

distance were the color of withered salmonberry
brush. When her eyes grew weary of the glare, she
closed them and then the motion of the train was
soothing.

With startling suddenness, the loud-speaker at the
end of their car announced their destination. "Next
stop—Santa Cecilia. Santa Cecilia next," said the
loud mechanical voice.

"Here we are," Mother said. "I have an idea it's
going to be warm out there. Better carry your coat,
dear."

The train slowed down and, as it did, Lisbeth felt
the courage draining out of her. Now there would
be new people. She was about to be left alone among
strangers. She pulled her gloves on nervously, forgetting the assurance her new clothes were supposed
to give her.

"Oh, Mother," she whispered, "how shall I act?
Whatever shall I do?"

"Why, do as you always do, dear," Mother said.
"Act like Lisbeth Craig of Hermit Bay."

The train came to a stop, and they went to the
end of the car and down the steps into the hot, dry
sunshine.

Mother, baggage checks in hand, retrieved Lisbeth's bags from the porter. Almost immediately

the train moved on, and Lisbeth saw that other girls and their mothers had got off from other cars. She was watching a man with two little girls who looked like twins, when a young woman approached Mother.

"You are Mrs. Craig," she said, smiling. "You were at St. Anne's for luncheon earlier this week. I am Janet Carey."

"Of course I remember you, Miss Carey." Mother held out her hand. "Lisbeth, this is Miss Carey, who will be your dramatics teacher."

Miss Carey had short hair almost as curly as Lisbeth's own. She wore a blue linen suit and no hat. She looked more like a girl than a teacher. "Lisbeth," she said, "you look just as I hoped you would! I'm so glad to meet a girl from Alaska."

She turned to Mother. "Don't worry about your bags. Beagle attends to the bags." She wrote Lisbeth's name on a bit of paper and slipped it under the handle of one of the bags. Then she left them to greet the others, and presently Lisbeth found herself being introduced to the Sherman twins and Mr. Sherman and to two girls older than herself, who were quite at ease and very informal. They were classmates, and had already been at St. Anne's Hall for two terms. Lisbeth thought their mothers not nearly as distinguished as her own, but she liked Mr. Sherman and the twins, who did not talk at all but made little curtsies when they were introduced.

Miss Carey found seats for all of them in the station wagon, which she herself drove. They took a gravel road that went past gardens and hedges and large houses half hidden in trees.

Behind her, Lisbeth could hear Jane Trenton and Louise Livermore talking in low voices and bursting continually into laughter, which they tried vainly to subdue. She felt a vague and unreasonable antagonism toward the two girls who had so much to talk and laugh about together. In front of her, the solemn little twins sat in the middle of the wide seat between Miss Carey and their father. Lisbeth felt hot and tight in her clothes. The air was dry and smelled of heat. She wanted to bolt, but there was no place to bolt to.

"We'll be there in a few minutes now," Mother said. "The grounds are beautiful. You'll love the flowers."

But Lisbeth was ready to throw in all the flowers in California for one rainy day in the Narrow Arm, with the green salt water at her feet. She squirmed in her seat and said nothing. They turned off the road and entered a long avenue of trees, at the end of which stood a great rambling building with wings reaching out on either side. It was an old building and, except for its size and the cross above its entrance, it was more like a house than a school. The road circled under a porte-cochere, with a big bed of white and pink petunias in the center of the circle. The building had a friendly look. Wide steps led up to a small porch and the impressive double doors with a fanlight above them. A trumpet vine climbed over the side of the porch, its heavy pink blossoms hanging in the heat.

"I like the building, don't you?" Mother asked.

"Yes," Lisbeth answered in a small voice.

When Miss Carey stopped the station wagon in front of the steps, she paused before getting out and looked down at the two little girls beside her. "In a day or two you'll feel at home here," she told them. "It won't take long for the strangeness to wear off."

They hid their heads against each other, and their father answered for them. "They'll be shy at first," he explained, as he opened the door on his side. "Come on, kids," he coaxed.

Lisbeth felt sorry for the twins, because they were so young that they did not know how to hide their feelings. As she got out of the station wagon, she kept her eyes averted from the two girls who came out after her, still laughing.

"Well, Jane," one of them giggled, "here we are —back at the salt mines."

"Don't take it too hard," Jane answered. "Mother'll come and bail us out for a week end now and then. Won't you, Moms?"

The door was opened by a maid in black, wearing a tiny white apron and cap. They all entered a big hall with a stairway rising at the far end. It was shadowy and cool. A huge bunch of yellow chrysanthemums stood on a table near the entrance to a reception room at the left. On the opposite side was a heavy paneled door with a small brass plate on which was engraved *Bishop Hastings*. That must be the bishop's office, just as Mother had said. From the stairway landing, St. George in armor, helmet in hand, gazed serenely down upon them from his wide gold frame.

The girl called Louise turned and said, "We'll be seeing you," as she followed her friend and their mothers down the hall. The Shermans and the Craigs were ushered into the reception room. The twins sat with their father on an uncomfortable Victorian settee. Mother and Lisbeth took chairs close together. They had hardly got settled when there was a rustling sound at the door. Mr. Sherman got to his feet. The twins' faces became more solemn than ever, and Mother, too, stood up. Lisbeth stood beside her, feeling her heart quicken as the headmistress came into the room.

Lisbeth's first impression was that here was authority itself. Miss Townsend moved among them with dignity and poise, but she was somehow separate from them. She did not seem to wear her clothes; she seemed to be encased in them. She spoke precisely, with a low, expressive voice. Queen Victoria must have entered a room like that and disposed of people with the same confident and commanding air. In a moment the house mother came in, and in a quite natural way the Sherman family vanished with this pleasant grandmotherly person, whose name was Mrs. Wiley.

"The poor little girls lost their mother last summer," Miss Townsend explained when they were gone. "We prefer not to take children under ten years for boarding students, but we have made an exception for Mr. Sherman. Our Mrs. Wiley has a real talent in caring for the little girls."

"I'm sure she has," Mother agreed.

Miss Townsend now directed her attention upon Lisbeth. "We are glad you have come, Lisbeth," she said. "You are our only girl from Alaska. I am sure you will do that country credit." She smiled.

Lisbeth, sitting stiffly on the edge of her chair, murmured an unsmiling thank-you. Miss Townsend had spoken of Alaska as though it were a foreign country. She went on to talk to Lisbeth about the ideals and aims of St. Anne's Hall, telling her that her roommate and the other "old" girls would help her to become accustomed to the rules and the activities of the school.

"Formal education is very pleasant and stimulating once you get the swing of it," she said. "If anything puzzles or troubles you, feel perfectly free to consult with your hall teacher. That is what she is there for."

Lisbeth listened as attentively as she could, knowing all the while that time was passing and Mother would have to leave soon to catch the return train to San Francisco. When the headmistress paused, she said, "I'll remember, Miss Townsend," but it did not sound like her own voice.

They talked a little longer about traveling and the weather, and then it was almost time for Mother to go. Miss Townsend went with them to the office, where the school secretary filled in a card and gave it to Lisbeth to sign. Mother left some money with the secretary, and Lisbeth learned that she was to have a bankbook and draw checks on her money. She took the little checkbook and looked at it doubtfully.

"Lisbeth has never handled money," Mother explained. "You see, where we live it is not necessary."

"Really!" exclaimed the headmistress. "Then indeed you live in the Garden of Eden."

There was real warmth and wonder in her voice, which Lisbeth detected immediately. It made her feel a degree less timid of this personage, her headmistress.

The appearance of Miss Carey, who was ready to leave to meet the northbound train, brought their conversation to an end. With her was a tall dark girl whom Lisbeth first mistook for a teacher. She was Gertrude Lee, a student of music who was to graduate that year. It was explained that Lisbeth's roommate, Dorothy Clayton, had not yet come, and Gertrude was to be her "big sister" until she arrived.

Mother turned toward Lisbeth as they walked on down the hall. "Darling, the time has gone so fast!" She went on in a low voice. "I'm so proud of you, Lisbeth. I shall tell Dad how splendid you are." She put her arm around her daughter and they walked slowly after the others. "Good-by, dear. I shall miss you. You'll write often, very often, won't you?"

Lisbeth had her jaws clamped together to hold back the tears. She had steeled herself for this, but now that it was happening she needed a minute to compose herself. She nodded her head vigorously.

"I'll tell Robbie to be sure to find time to come and see you soon," Mother went on hurriedly. "Then at the holidays Dad and I shall come and take you home for Christmas."

Lisbeth could feel Mother's distress at the parting. "I'll be all right, Mother," she said bravely. "Don't you worry. I'll write often. I . . . I won't forget."

They were in the great hall with the chrysanthemums and St. George again. The maid in the little cap was holding open the big door. Outside, shadows had fallen across the lawn and the petunia bed. Miss Townsend was bidding Mother good-by. Then Mother kissed Lisbeth and squeezed her hard before she quickly followed Miss Carey out. The big door closed with a soft thud, and Lisbeth quivered as she stood staring at its gleaming panels.

C H A P T E R 6

LISBETH HEARD Miss Townsend's firm voice. "Gertrude Lee will go up with you, Lisbeth. I am sorry that Dorothy Clayton has not arrived, but others have come and Gertrude will see that you meet them."

Now it had started. Lisbeth turned quickly away from the doors. She was alert and excited in a fearful sort of way. She had felt this way once when Dad was bringing them into harbor after dark. That had been a night when you could not see anything at all, when rain poured through the darkness and you could not even pick up the contours of the mountains to guide you. She had stood at one of the wheelhouse windows, trying with all her senses to make out how close to land they were. Now, alone and in an unfamiliar place for the first time in her life, she fairly bristled with caution and alertness. She thanked Miss Townsend. Then she walked down the hall with Gertrude Lee.

"I'll tell you about the stairs as we go up," Gertrude said, smiling.

For the first time in her life Lisbeth forced her face to smile. "Is there something special about the stairs?" she asked, her lips stiff with her effort.

"Indeed there is," the older girl answered. "This is the main stairway. It has a tradition."

As they started up the stairs, Lisbeth glanced at the painting of St. George above them. The tranquil eyes seemed to gaze encouragingly into her own.

"We call this stairway St. George's Hill," Gertrude went on. "It's used only by upperclassmen and members of the faculty. On Commencement Day, after the exercises when the seniors have been given their diplomas, all the sophomores who have made their grades run into the hall from the court and dash up St. George's Hill."

Lisbeth listened politely but said nothing.

Gertrude looked at her as they reached the top of the carpeted stairway. "It's really quite exciting," she said. "You've just become an upperclassman and you feel thrilled to be using the front stairway."

"What stairway do the . . . the others use?" Lisbeth asked.

"The one that comes down near the study-hall door in the north wing—that's the plebs' stairway."

Lisbeth did not know what pleb meant. She felt too shy to ask, so she said nothing.

"When you get to be a senior, you love all the traditions of St. Anne's," Gertrude told her. "At first some of the girls pretend to hate them, but when they're ready to graduate they remember the fun they had when they were plebs. That's what we call the underclassmen."

They had reached the upper hall, where the sun poured in through three windows at one end and corridors led off into the wings. Lisbeth felt stifled in her wool dress and her arm was damp under the coat she carried.

As they turned down the first corridor to their right, they heard squeals of laughter and shouts of greeting going on in the rooms. Jane Trenton, one of the two girls Lisbeth had met in the station wagon, leaned out of a doorway in front of them and shouted at the top of her lungs, "Is Clarissa here yet? Has anyone seen Clarissa Jones?"

Then, as heads appeared along the corridor, she spotted Lisbeth coming down the hall. "Well, here's our silent partner," she cried good-naturedly. "Are you going to live in South Hall?"

From the opposite door girls' faces appeared in a bunch, looking out curiously.

"For heaven's sake, Jane! You'll have Miss White on us if you keep up that shouting," one of them warned.

"Oh, how *dreadful*," Jane cried in exaggerated dismay.

With that they all burst into shrieks of laughter. Lisbeth felt herself congeal inwardly and begin to perspire outwardly.

"This is Lisbeth Craig, girls," Gertrude said in her low voice. Then, as the laughter stopped as suddenly as it had begun, she introduced the girls by name. Betty Gray and Anne Barton, Marylin Coombs and Peg Smith and Jeanne Avers. The names whirled through Lisbeth's head. When someone said, "Hello, Elizabeth," she explained that her name was Lisbeth.

Betty Gray was a big, athletic girl in whose room they were all waiting for the arrival of her pleb. "I thought at first you were my pleb," she said with a friendly smile. "But mine's got a different name—Sally Reynolds."

"You won't have any trouble recognizing yours, Betty," Jane cut in from her door across the corridor. "Yours will have two heads."

Again they all screamed with laughter. Even Gertrude chuckled at the irrepressible Jane. As she turned to lead Lisbeth on, the door farthest down the corridor opened and a small, angular figure stepped out and stood silhouetted against the high arched window.

"Girls!" came a crisp, not unpleasant voice. "Girls, please lower your voices."

There followed an immediate silence.

Then Jane said, "It's my fault, Miss White. I'm sorry."

"First Day is difficult," said Miss White. "Please try to remember that you are indoors, Jane."

She stepped back into her room, and Lisbeth and Gertrude continued their walk toward it, pausing for more introductions on the way. Behind them, suppressed giggles and half-whispered words grew into a confused murmur.

Miss White was a dry little woman with her graying hair twisted in a tight bun on top of her head.

She gave Lisbeth's hand a firm clasp with her own cool, thin fingers and looked directly into her eyes through rimless bifocal glasses. "I am very glad to meet you, Lisbeth Craig," she said. "You must not think me a monster because I popped out like that just as you arrived."

Miss White looked like anything but a monster. She looked exactly like Lisbeth's conception of the way a teacher should look. "I'm glad to meet you, Miss White," she said, wishing her hand was as cool and dry as the teacher's.

"I hope you will continue to be glad," said Miss White. "I am your hall teacher—a sort of combination policeman and mother confessor. Let me see. . . ." She consulted a list on her desk. "You are to room in 12 with Dorothy Clayton. Dorothy should be here, but since she is not, perhaps Gertrude will help you unpack and tell you the few things you need to know on First Day."

"Of course," Gertrude assented.

Lisbeth wanted to protest that she could do her own unpacking and that she would enjoy doing it alone. But she remembered Long Paul's admonition to run at slow speed until she got her bearings, so she only said, "Thank you," and followed Gertrude into the hall.

South Hall made a right-angle turn in front of Miss White's room. Another high window was at the far end of the ell, and through it Lisbeth could see distant hills, spotted with clumps of live-oak trees. Gertrude showed her the shower room and lavatory, and a few doors farther on they came to Number 12. As Gertrude put her hand on the knob, Louise Livermore thrust her head out of the door opposite.

"Hi, Gertrude!" she cried. "Did you just get back? Are you in South Hall, too? I've already met Lisbeth Craig—at the station." She looked over her shoulder, as Gertrude responded to her greeting, with a casualness that missed being rude only because of her obvious intention of friendliness. "Come here and meet the people across the hall, Ellen," she said. "Ellen's my pleb," she told them.

Ellen Johnson was very blonde, with short pig-tails and white eyebrows that gave her round face a blank expression. She said, "Hello, Elizabeth."

Lisbeth looked into a pair of bland blue eyes. "My name is Lisbeth," she explained.

"That sounds like a nickname," Ellen declared flatly.

"It's an old name in our family," Lisbeth retorted, stiffening with annoyance.

"Sounds to me like a baby trying to say Elizabeth," Ellen argued stubbornly.

Gertrude was explaining to Louise that her own room was in North Hall. "Dorothy Clayton will be in 12 with Lisbeth. She's late arriving."

"No!" Louise exclaimed with a burst of laughter. "When we ran up St. George's Hill last June, Dot swore she would never do big-sister duty for a pleb. She said she was going to spend her whole summer recruiting new upperclassmen for St. Anne's, so she could have one to room with."

Lisbeth felt a drop of perspiration trickle down from under her hat as she backed toward the door of Number 12.

"Oh, Dorothy was joking," Gertrude said. "She doesn't mean half of what she says."

Lisbeth entered the room that was to be her home for the next three months with a feeling of foreboding. She thought she could not bear meeting any more girls, and she started to close the door.

"We leave the doors open on First Day," Gertrude explained. "It helps in getting acquainted and it helps the hall teacher to see who's come and who hasn't."

Lisbeth left the protecting door ajar. Tears suddenly smarted in her eyes. She clenched her teeth and fought them back.

"I'll bet you've got something cool to wear in your trunk," Gertrude said, looking at the luggage standing neatly in the middle of the room. "It's awfully warm today. Why don't you slip into a cool dress? I'll help hang your things in the closet while you change."

With an effort Lisbeth fought down her rebellious tears. She longed to get out of the wool dress that had been comfortable enough in San Francisco but was stifling in the heat of the valley.

"Does it matter which side of the room you have?" Gertrude asked, appearing not to notice her conflict.

Lisbeth looked around the room, furnished in halves with beds, dressers, desks, and closet doors exactly alike. Even the chairs were alike except in color. She threw her coat on the bed at the left. "No, it doesn't matter in the least," she said. "And I guess I *will* change my dress. I'm awfully hot." She got her keys out of her handbag and unlocked all of the luggage.

"We don't dress for dinner on First Day. Just anything cool will do," Gertrude told her. "Shall I put the dresses in your trunk away?"

A feeling of friendliness welled up in Lisbeth as

she peeled off her dress. "Oh, thank you, Gertrude," she said. "I'm afraid it's an awful bother. I'll be ready in a minute."

"I'll begin then," the older girl offered. She opened the little wardrobe trunk and turned back the blue dust covers. With exclamations of delight, she began taking out the dresses, skirts, and blouses and hanging them in the closet. "Lisbeth, your clothes are darling," she exclaimed.

Lisbeth had opened the big suitcase to find her moccasins. The checked taffeta dress was on top and she shook out the tissue paper that Mother had packed it in, remembering that just last night she had worn it to Uncle Jim's dinner party. Just last night! Ages of time seemed to have passed since then.

"What an adorable dress! Do let me hang it up." Gertrude took the dress and held it out to admire.

Lisbeth told Gertrude that the taffeta was her favorite dress but that she liked the sea-green shantung with the little white sailboats on it almost as well. Standing in her slip and stocking feet, she felt the quiver leaving her knees and she began to calm down.

"Do put this one on, Lisbeth." Gertrude held out the brown linen dress with its short-sleeved bolero and long-sleeved white blouse. "This looks so cool."

Lisbeth got into the dress and buttoned the white blouse up to its round collar. Then she put on the bolero. "There are some brown shoes in one of these cases," she said, searching for and finally finding the light shoes with flat wedge soles. "Mother said these were especially for hot days."

As the girls unpacked, new arrivals kept coming. Gail Hathaway, the school tennis champion, and her pleb, Georgia Marsdon, moved in on one side of Lisbeth's room, and Kathie Schmidt and Harriet Keene took possession of the room on the other side. By now the door of Number 12 stood wide open. Lisbeth wrote her room number on the tag on her empty trunk, and she and Gertrude carried it out and placed it beside her door.

"Beagle will take the trunk and bags to the store-room in the morning," Gertrude explained.

Ellen and Louise were in the hall, talking to new arrivals. "Oh, look," Ellen said. "She's got a new dress on already."

"Oh, leave her alone," Louise said impatiently. "Don't mind my pleb," she explained to all of them. "She doesn't know any better."

Lisbeth retreated to her room in the laughter that followed. Later, when a bell chimed through South

Hall announcing dinner, she was cool and outwardly calm. She had met everyone who came into the ell during the afternoon, and had responded to the casual greetings in her own old-fashioned, formal manner. She had made the correction each time her name was pronounced incorrectly. There had not been a single moment when she could sit down and think and try to find her soundings. Her wardrobe had been examined and questions asked with a directness that shocked her. As they all flocked down the corridor, she was ravenous with hunger and at the same time longing for night, when she could close her door and be alone.

CHAPTER 7

LISBETH WALKED CLOSE to Gertrude, who seemed like an oasis of quiet in the chattering flock. At the top of the stairs they met more girls coming from North Hall. Jane Trenton rushed forward to embrace a graceful gypsy of a girl whom she greeted as Clarissa Jones. As they descended the stairs, Jane exhorted the plebs to "tread lightly on these hallowed stairs," because after today they would use the linoleum-covered, metal-edged stairs becoming to their station in life.

"I daresay we can endure it," Jane's pleb, Anne Barton, replied.

Jane giggled. "Now look here, Anne, my little pleb! The Regal T. rules the downstairs hall and no noise is allowed. Don't you dare make me laugh!" She finished in a loud whisper.

Lisbeth was about to ask who was the Regal T., when it occurred to her that it could be no other than Miss Townsend. She wondered if there was anything at all that Jane took seriously. To her own amusement, voices were lowered and steps slowed in the downstairs hall as they moved into the south wing. About halfway down, a wide doorway opened into an anteroom, with the big dining room beyond. Some members of the faculty were already waiting in the anteroom, and the girls stopped there also, politely greeting the teachers and introducing the plebs. They stopped talking suddenly, as they detected a hush in the corridor outside.

In a moment Miss Townsend made her entrance, and with her was a big man in clerical clothes. His gray hair stood up stiff and straight on his majestic head. His eyebrows shot upward from the corners of his eyes and he had a big beak of a nose.

"The bishop!" Jane cried in a delighted whisper. "The bishop's here for dinner!"

The big man turned and looked at her. "Oh, there you are, Jane," he said, pausing. "I thought I missed something out there in the hall," he went on, as Jane blushed with happy confusion. "No noise— no giggles. I'm glad to see you back, Jane." He beamed at her affectionately and went on into the dining room.

Lisbeth sniffed the air. To her surprise, she detected the delicate fragrance of cigar smoke. It brought a wave of homesickness and a sudden feeling of love for the bishop. He stood out like a lighthouse on a rocky coast—a man in the house, and a kind one at that. Lisbeth wondered if she would ever get to know the bishop as well as Jane knew him.

The teachers followed the headmistress and the bishop into the dining room, and then the old girls and their new students flocked in. Soon all of the tables were surrounded by girls and teachers, standing behind their chairs. When the room grew quiet, the bishop bowed his head and said grace.

Then there was a scraping of chairs and everyone sat down. The round tables each seated six girls and one teacher. Before picking up their spoons and starting on the chilled grapefruit, the new girls were introduced to the teacher. At Lisbeth's table, Miss Langley, the teacher of history, presided. She was a large, stern woman, wearing two strings of antique

beads and small, old-fashioned earrings. She ac-
knowledged the introductions with a strained
smile and a careful repetition of each name. During the meal she asked each girl where her home
was.

When Lisbeth's turn came and she replied that
she was from the southeast coast of Alaska, there
followed a brief pause as the teacher bent an interested gaze upon her.

"Ah, yes," Miss Langley said, "Seward's folly!"

A repressed titter went round the table, and Lisbeth felt the color creep into her face. She had never
heard of Seward's folly.

"Of course it has turned out to be anything but
that," Miss Langley hastened to say, with a piercing
glance at the smiling girls. "Alaska is a very valuable
possession and an interesting place, I am sure, in a
scenic way."

She paused again, as though expecting a reply, but
Lisbeth kept her eyes on her plate and said nothing,
hoping the talk would center elsewhere.

But Miss Langley was not so easily turned aside.
"Which city is your home, Lisbeth?" she persisted.

Lisbeth looked up. "We are near Juneau," she
answered, as conclusively as she could. "About a
hundred miles by water."

"Why water?" one of the girls asked. "Don't they have roads in Alaska?"

Balked for a moment by the direct questions, Lisbeth hesitated. Then she remembered a description of the coast in one of her own school geographies. "The coast is very mountainous," she quoted, "deeply indented with bays and fiords, making roads impractical." To her embarrassment, she saw the amused glances of her schoolmates. "We use planes or boats when we go anywhere," she added.

"I suppose you set sail to go to the movies a hundred miles away?" the same girl inquired with mock innocence.

"What are you talking about, Jinny?" Jane Trenton demanded. "They don't have movies in Alaska. They have powwows in igloos. Right?" She beamed good-naturedly at Lisbeth.

But Jinny's question had been impudent, and Lisbeth knew it. She was too angry to take up Jane's joke.

Miss Langley quickly took the conversation in hand by explaining that certain Eskimos used igloos, and from there she went on to other types of primitive dwellings in the South Seas and elsewhere. By the time the meal was ended, Lisbeth had the impression that Miss Langley, at least, really suspected that she did live in an igloo or a smokehouse or perhaps an Aleutian hut. She was relieved when the maids carried out the last of the dishes and the bishop stood up to greet the school.

He stood grasping the knobs on the back of his chair, as he looked at the faces turned toward him. He took time to smile upon all of them, until even the faces of the Sherman twins lit up and they looked at each other happily. When he spoke, he welcomed them so warmly to St. Anne's that Lisbeth felt the glow of it in her own breast. He spoke especially to the new girls and told funny little jokes that made them all laugh. Then, searching the tables to find them, he mentioned each senior by name and wished them all success and happiness in their last year at the school. Amidst a clapping of hands he left the room with Miss Townsend, and the others followed after them.

At the top of the stairs Lisbeth turned to Gertrude. "Please don't feel that you must come back to my room with me," she said. "I shall finish unpacking and go to bed. I can get on quite all right now."

"If you're sure you won't feel lonely," Gertrude answered hesitantly. "I do have a few things to attend to."

"Oh, not a bit," Lisbeth declared. "Thank you, Gertrude. Thank you very much."

The girls bade each other good night and Lisbeth sped down South Hall and into the ell. She wanted to get to her room and try to think things out. The girls were moving slowly now, lingering before each other's doors, asking and answering interminable questions. She passed them swiftly, hardly aware of the glances that followed her. She gained her room before anyone else had turned into the ell. Leaving the door only a few inches ajar, she walked to one of the windows, drew back the curtain, and stood looking out, trying to compose the muddle of her thoughts and feelings.

Across the wide court were the many windows of the north ell and, as she watched, lights came on here and there and she could see girls moving about in the rooms. For a moment it was quiet, and she sighed and stood listening to the silence until she became aware of the tinkling of water down in the court. Below her a fountain scattered water from the hands of a marble nymph. In the twilight she could see pale water lilies blooming in the pond around it. The green of the shrubbery and the lawn was growing dim in the dusk, but the white paving of the senior walk that circled within the square showed clearly. She felt that she could never endure all the years that must pass before she would be a senior.

Again there came a babble of voices in the hall, and Lisbeth drew back reluctantly and crossed the room to switch on the lights. She drew the blinds and began to finish her unpacking. She put her yellow candlewick robe and a pair of blue cotton pajamas on the bed, and her white doeskin moccasins beside it. Gertrude had told her that a bell would chime at eight-thirty, and then she could close her door and prepare for bed. At nine o'clock all the lights would be turned off except in the seniors' rooms. She wound her little clock and put it on the desk to be set when the bell chimed.

As she unpacked her bags, she put her keepsakes and the pictures of Mother and Dad on the dresser, and then she found Uncle Jim's present and two other packages Mother had hidden in her suitcase. She lined them up on the desk to await the longed-for chime of the bell. Then she stiffened and looked quickly toward the door. There was giggling outside and someone said, "Oh, come on."

The door was flung back and a horde of girls burst into her room. "We're from North Hall," Jinny Clarke announced. "We're calling on people."

"Oh . . . oh . . . please come in," Lisbeth said, overwhelmed by the number in her room. She remembered Jinny's mocking questions at the table, as she tried to join the laughter that followed.

"Isn't Dot here yet?" Jinny asked. "Miss Townsend will be furious at her when she does come, for neglecting her pleb like this."

"Oh, I don't mind," Lisbeth hastened to say.

"Maybe not," Jinny rejoined, "but the Regal T. does." Then she turned to the others. "Girls," she went on in the manner of an army sergeant, "this is *Lis*beth—L-i-s-beth, get it?—Craig from Alaska." She caught sight of the moccasins beside the bed. "See?" she said, picking them up. "Lisbeth is a dead-pan Eskimo straight from an igloo, like I told you."

"Those are Thlinkit moccasins," Lisbeth said as coolly as she could. "The Eskimos wear a different kind of footgear."

"Oh, lookit! Look at these! What are they?" Someone had discovered the keepsakes on her dresser.

Lisbeth explained, with an inner feeling of pride, that the big tooth came from a bear weighing seventeen hundred pounds that her Uncle Jim had shot when he was a young man. The talons were from an eagle her brother had shot, because it had carried away one of the kittens. The little totem was a Thlinket carving, and all the figures meant something. Before she had finished explaining the totem, the girls had lost interest in it. They seated themselves on the beds and chairs and looked at her curiously. "That totem'll give Dot morbid dreams," one of them said. "She hates ugly things."

"This is a cute robe," said another, pulling the yellow robe from under the girl who had sat down on it. "Can you buy things like this in Alaska?"

Lisbeth rescued her robe and pajamas. "I'll hang them up out of the way," she explained.

"*Do* they have stores in Alaska? I mean smart stores," her questioner insisted.

"There are stores in the towns, of course," Lisbeth answered, appalled by their ignorance. "I don't know whether you would call them smart or not."

"Tell them how far you are from the stores, Lisbeth, and how you get there," Jinny prompted.

Lisbeth looked at her, realizing that she was the ringleader of this group of callers and that she must have been amusing them with stories made up out of the dinner-table questioning. She was too resentful to make light of the attempt to draw her out, and did not know how to turn the joke.

"What does it matter here, how far a store is from

home?" she asked. "It doesn't matter there." Her heart began to flutter as she felt the attitude of the girls change from expectancy to hostility. One of them got up and yawned, but before she could speak, a small pale girl said in a bored voice, "What they really want to know, Lisbeth, is where you got your clothes. Louise was talking about them coming up the stairs."

"Why . . . why . . . we shopped in San Francisco on the way down," Lisbeth said with surprise.

"Did you *arrive* in San Francisco in a parka?" Jinny inquired. "Since Lexy has introduced the candid attitude, let's have a look." She opened the closet door wide, and there was a moment of silence while the girls looked with unashamed curiosity at her new wardrobe.

"Why, everything's new," Jinny went on. "What *did* you wear in Alaska?" She was now frankly curious.

Lisbeth was outraged. Furious with anger, she could think of no reply except to order them all out of her room. But some inner wisdom kept her silent. She stood looking at her inquisitor, saying nothing.

The girls moved uneasily away from the closet. Out in the hall, a bell chimed five times once and then again. The girls started for the door. The one who had yawned, yawned again, stretching her arms above her head. "Well—First Day's—over at last," she remarked.

Some of them murmured, "Good night," as they went out. With uneasy bravado Jinny Clarke said, "Good night, L-i-s-beth," as she departed among them. They all filed out except the small pale girl, who lingered behind. Lisbeth remained silent, near to tears.

"My name is Alexandria Burke," the girl said. "They call me Lexy, for short. I'm not staying behind because I particularly like you. It always takes time to decide about people. I'm staying because I don't like flocking around with the sheep."

When Lisbeth said nothing, she went on. "Don't let Jinny Clarke get you. She's always trying to make someone squirm."

"Thank you. I . . . I won't." Lisbeth tried to keep her voice from breaking.

Lexy got up languidly and went to the door. "She didn't really get the better of you, you know," she said with apparent satisfaction. "She thought you would be stupid enough to brag about Alaska and give her an opening to razz you." She paused at the door and turned her candid gray eyes on Lisbeth. "Good night, Lisbeth Craig," she said.

"Good night," Lisbeth murmured, as Lexy went out and closed the door.

Lisbeth walked about the room, nervously straightening the spread on Dorothy's bed and her own and replacing the chairs. She was burning with anger. Why hadn't she told them that she wore a blanket at home and traveled in a bear hide! Why did she have to get so confused and scared? "L-i-s-beth, get it? Craig!" She silently mimicked Jinny Clarke. If only she had the wits to think of retorts when she needed them. If she could only be bantering and smooth like Robbie, she could get on with all of them and they'd never know the difference. But she couldn't be like that. And now she had forgotten to set her clock and pretty soon it would be time for lights out. She undressed and put on her robe, longing for a cool shower. But when she got to the shower room other girls were waiting, and she hastily washed in a basin rather than undergo the ordeal of waiting and talking.

Back in her room, she stood in front of her desk, looking absently at the three little packages lying there and thinking of all the things she *should* have said and done during the day. Lonely and grim, she finally chose the tiny box Uncle Jim had given her and sat down on the edge of her bed to open it. Inside, nestled on cotton, was a little silver owl. On a card in the top of the box she read, "An owlful of wisdom for my baby." It was almost like Uncle Jim talking. Tremulously she took the silver pin out of the box and held it in her hand. It was an uncommon, lovely little owl of fine workmanship. She pinned it on her pajama coat and looked in the mirror. She saw the unhappiness on the face in the mirror, and she straightened up and thrust out her jaw with such sternness that the face gazed back at her with startled eyes. "An owlful of wisdom!" She smiled in spite of herself, looking at the little owl on her coat.

Out in the hall the bell chimed out its notes, repeating them twice. Lisbeth made a grab for her clock and set it at nine. Lights out at nine, Gertrude had said. She dashed across the room and snapped off the lights. The room, with the blinds drawn, was plunged into immediate darkness with only a dim rectangle of light in the transom above the door. Slowly she groped her way to the windows and raised the blinds. Across the court she could see girls raising blinds and crossing their rooms to turn off the lights. A faint glow came from the court below, and the tinkle of water in the fountain drifted up on the warm air. Her eyes grew accustomed to the darkness and she could make out the objects in the room as she stood listening, feeling strange in this building where everyone did the same thing at the sound of a bell. It seemed like yesterday or a week ago that the door had shut on Mother, but she realized with a pang that Mother was traveling back to Hermit Bay now and all those miles were stretching out between them.

Too desolate to get into bed, she went to the desk and picked up her two remaining packages. She could tell by the smell and the shape that one was a bottle of lotion like Mother's, and she put it on her dresser to open in the morning. The other was smaller and she could not guess what it was. Softly she placed a chair in front of the door and, standing on tiptoe on it, she opened the little box. Holding it up to the light in the transom, she saw that it held a wrist watch—a little silver watch on a leather band. She was taken completely by surprise and was still staring at it when she heard a soft knock at her door. Like a mink surprised at its feeding, she stood perfectly still with her head raised, trying to sense who this could be. The door opened a crack.

"Lisbeth Craig? May I come in, Lisbeth?" Miss White's voice was crisp, even when she spoke softly.

With a flash of alarm at being caught out of bed,

Lisbeth stepped down from the chair and pulled it out of the way.

"Yes . . . yes . . . of course, Miss White," she stammered.

The door opened, letting a wide bar of soft light fall across the room.

"I . . . I . . . was trying to look at my . . . my new watch. It's a present," she finished lamely.

"A new watch?" Miss White came in and switched on the desk light. "Bring it here, child, and look at it. I know you'll never get to sleep with a present like that waiting to be seen."

Recovering from her surprise, Lisbeth held the watch under the light. "Oh, it's a beauty," Miss White exclaimed.

"It's got a card in the box. Oh . . . it's from Dad!" Reading the card, Lisbeth was so full of emotion she could not say another word. She read: "Don't never turn to round a point until you come to it. With love, Dad." With a shaky laugh, she showed the card to Miss White. Then she felt tears running down her cheeks while she laughed, and she tried to stop them and failed.

"It has a private meaning, hasn't it?" the teacher said, pretending not to notice the tears. "Or perhaps I'm dull and don't get it," she went on. "First

Day always leaves me more dead than alive." She
went to the door and closed it and Lisbeth found a
handkerchief and blew her nose.

"Suppose we sit down and you tell me what it
means." Miss White drew a chair near the bed.
"Why not jump into bed while you tell me?"

Lisbeth turned back the bed covers and curled up
on the sheet. The sudden tears had stopped, but her
eyes were still wet and she kept them on the watch
in her hand as she explained the card.

"We have a wonderful skipper named Long Paul,
who taught me how to steer a boat when I was very
little," she said. "The first thing you learn when
you're steering a boat is never to make a turn until
you're abreast of your channel." She looked at Miss
White to see if this point was clear.

The teacher nodded rather doubtfully.

"Long Paul says many wise things," Lisbeth went
on, "but sometimes he says them in a funny way. On
that day he told me to look ahead at a point we were
supposed to go around." She paused and took a
deep breath to steady her voice. "He said," she continued, "he said, 'Don't never turn to round a point
until you come to it.' "

"Oh, I see!" Miss White cried triumphantly.

"Your father is telling you to proceed intelligently—see your way before you go ahead."

"Yes!" Lisbeth gave her an appreciative look. "In our family we say that when any of us gets too hasty." Almost before she finished the sentence, she felt herself relax like a balloon with the air going out of it, and though she tried clenching her teeth together she could not check the yawn that overcame her. "Oh, please excuse me!" she said.

Miss White got up. "Of course, Lisbeth. I dropped in just to say good night and see how you survived First Day. I think you've done better than I have." She smiled at Lisbeth and moved toward the door, turning off the desk light as she went. "In the morning we go to chapel before breakfast," she said as she reached the door. "Sit anywhere you want at breakfast. By noon the tables will be assigned. Good night, Lisbeth."

"Good night, Miss White," Lisbeth replied. "Thank you for coming in."

When the door closed, she stretched out in the cool sheets, thinking of Hermit Bay and the boats. Vaguely she remembered that she ought to be charting the rocks and the shoals of St. Anne's—there were so many of them. But she went to sleep before she could begin.

C H A P T E R 8

THE NEXT MORNING, to Lisbeth's surprise, Jane Trenton came to her door. "Want to go to chapel with Anne and me?" she asked.

"Thank you," Lisbeth said, "if it won't be a bother. I can get on all right, you know."

"Of course you can," Jane replied. "But it won't be much fun. Come along."

As they left the room she went on, "I hope it's the bishop this morning. Dean North is at our chapel usually. He is sweet, but I don't love him the way I love Bishop Hastings."

They met Anne at Jane's door and walked around to the plebs' stairs together, with Jane pretending to be doing a gracious favor by condescending to use their stairs. A little girl came clattering down after them.

"Jane—oh, Jane!" she cried. "Can I go along with you?"

Jane turned around and hugged her. "Marty Evans! I missed you yesterday in all the rush. Anne, Lisbeth, this is little Marty."

The little girl appeared to be nine or ten years old. She had a round face topped with short black curls, and eyes almost as dark, that danced with life. Her cheeks were red as apples and she seemed to be bursting with eagerness. She beamed at Lisbeth. "You look both little and big," she remarked, taking hold of her hand and smiling at Anne as though she wanted to include everybody.

Lisbeth held onto the plump little hand, feeling that whatever Marty meant by looking "both little and big," it must be something good. They walked together past the dining room and into the downstairs ell of the south wing. At the end of the ell Gothic doors stood open and they could see the altar, soft in the candlelight. A few girls and teachers were already in the chapel, some kneeling and some sit-

ting in the pews. Lisbeth had not been in a church
since her baptism. She looked uncertainly at Jane
as they went in.

"Follow me, and do exactly what I do," Jane
whispered. "I *thought* you were a heathen."

Lisbeth felt an impulse to laugh, but it did not
get even as far as a smile because of her fear that she
might make some conspicuous mistake. She walked
so close behind Jane that she nearly bumped her
when she paused to make a genuflection before entering the pew. Lisbeth followed her awkwardly,
kneeling down and getting up when she did. Little
Marty remained kneeling longer. When she slid
back into the seat, she reached for a prayer book,
opened it at the right place, and handed it to Lisbeth. Organ music began softly drifting through
the little chapel and Lisbeth saw that it was Gertrude
Lee who was playing. Almost every pew was filled
when the bishop came in, wearing surplice and stole,
and everyone stood up to sing the opening hymn.

When the short service was over, Lisbeth came out
of the chapel much moved. It was a shock to her to
see the girls change instantly from their quiet mood
to the chattering, flippant one she feared and could
not share.

After breakfast there was time for making their

beds, putting their rooms in order, and finishing any
unpacking they yet had to do. At ten o'clock, at the
chime of a bell, they were all to go to the study hall
to be officially welcomed by Miss Townsend.

The hall was full when Lisbeth got there and most
of the girls were seated at the school desks. There
were many strange faces she had not seen the day
before, and she saw with dread that girls were sitting
two on a seat at the big desks in the rear half of the
long room. No single seats were left. She walked
slowly toward the rear, too shy to take one of the
half seats with someone strange to her. Yet she would
have to sit somewhere, and she looked over the
crowded room with a feeling of panic. Most of the
girls she had met were sitting with their roommates.
Gertrude Lee was across the room with another
senior. Near the middle aisle there was a slight
commotion where Betty Gray was trying to talk to
a girl on the other side of the room. Betty caught
sight of Lisbeth and signaled for her to come. With
a surge of relief Lisbeth hastened toward her.

"Lisbeth, would you mind sitting here?" Betty
asked. "I'm dying to talk to Pat." She was out of
the seat before there was time to answer. "This is
my pleb, Sally Reynolds. She's from Arizona—fasci-
nating! Thanks a lot, Lisbeth."

Lisbeth looked at Sally and sat down as near to the edge of the seat as she could. Sally was a thin, plain little girl with mouse-colored hair and gray-blue eyes.

"There's lots of room," she said. "You'll get bumped if you hang out in the aisle. Are you new, too?"

"Yes," Lisbeth said, sliding cautiously over on the seat. "My roommate hasn't come yet."

"I heard them talking about it," Sally answered. "You're from Alaska, aren't you?"

Lisbeth felt herself bristle. "Yes," she replied.

"I think that's wonderful," Sally said sincerely. "I hope you'll tell me about it some day and show me your things. I live away out in the country too, on a ranch." She stopped talking as a slow rush of movement swept through the big room. The girls were all getting to their feet, old girls hushing new girls, and all looking toward the platform at the front.

Lisbeth and Sally stood, turning the seat up so that they would occupy no more than their share of the aisle. Miss Townsend entered and now stood facing them from the platform. Gradually the rustling of seats stopped. Then the headmistress said, "You may be seated, girls," and the noise of desk

seats going down and the general blur of sound
filled the room again and again died into silence.

Then Miss Townsend talked about St. Anne's
Hall, its aims and its rules, and the things she hoped
the girls would gain from their years at the school.
Lisbeth found herself listening intently to the beautiful pronunciation of the words and feeling the
depth of their meaning.

Miss Townsend went on to say that she was aware
that the rules of St. Anne's were subject to human
weakness and therefore subject to change, but they
had been thoughtfully made. If any student felt that
a rule was unjust, it was her duty to discuss the matter with her teacher-adviser. She spoke of the importance of education, and urged them to take part
in the many activities St. Anne's offered.

When she had finished, all the girls stood up as
she left the study hall. Then Miss White indicated
lists of names on a blackboard, and explained that
each girl should find there the name of her teacher-
adviser and meet with her at once in the room
assigned.

"We both have Miss Carey," Sally whispered.
"I'm glad."

Lisbeth looked at the names on the blackboard
listed under Miss Carey's and saw her own and

Sally's. "I'm glad, too," she murmured. She felt comfortable with Sally Reynolds, but there on the list was that awful Ellen Johnson, too.

"Girls, please remember to lower your voices when you go out," Miss White advised. "The halls can become bedlam if we all shout."

Someone nearby in the crowd mimicked her way of speaking and subdued giggles spread. Lisbeth felt a quick resentment. She liked Miss White. She tried to see who it was that had ridiculed her, but she could not find the girl in the confusion. She hated moving in a crowd like this. It made her want to strike out right and left and race through to find an open place. She glanced at Sally, who was at her side, and saw that Sally's face was set and her eyes a little panicky. They squeezed out through the crowded door together.

In the hallway some of the girls moved rapidly away toward the classrooms, but in the corner where the plebs' stairs came down a group of them were squirming with repressed laughter, holding their hands over their mouths and leaning on each other's shoulders. Lisbeth could see Jinny Clarke standing against the wall, her chest stuck out and her stomach pulled way in, as she caricatured Miss Townsend's figure and voice. "We are awaah that the rules of

Sun t'Anne's are subject to hewman weakness," she was saying, darting birdlike glances at her listeners, who were helpless with laughter.

Lisbeth hurried past, horrified at the disrespect and cruelty. She had been much impressed by what Miss Townsend had said. Upset and unhappy, she went along with Sally to Room 10, where they were to meet Miss Carey.

Miss Carey greeted each girl as she came in, and handed her a little notebook and a pencil.

"It's a good idea to write everything down at first," she told them. "It helps to remember."

Miss Carey went on talking in a friendly informal manner, and Lisbeth found herself feeling that she had been lucky to get into Miss Carey's group.

"It's not easy to become acquainted sitting in rows in a classroom," the young teacher said. "We'll meet soon in my room and get to know each other better. Today," she continued, "we'll just have time enough to copy the class schedules. This afternoon I'll meet you in this room after you have got your books from the office, and then I'll assign your gymnasium lockers. If there's any doubt concerning classes, we can straighten it out so that there will be no confusion tomorrow."

The girls began to copy their schedules and subjects of study. There was one list headed "Electives," from which each girl was to choose two.

"It is wise to give careful thought to your choice of electives," Miss Carey advised. "It's your chance to study something you really love."

Lisbeth copied down her classes with considerable interest. Algebra with Miss White, Latin with Miss Elkhorn, ancient history with Miss Langley, and English with Miss Meadows. There were study periods between classes, and twice each week there was an hour for gymnasium. She chose drama and interpretive dancing for her electives, because Miss Carey taught them.

The girls left one by one as they finished, some of them stopping to discuss their electives on the way out. Lisbeth was the last to finish and as she started to leave, Miss Carey called her to the desk.

"Are you getting on all right, Lisbeth, without any roommate to help you?" she asked.

"Yes, thank you," Lisbeth answered.

Miss Carey looked at her and smiled, as she rose from the desk and gathered up her things. "I think you are a very brave girl, Lisbeth," she said, "coming from such a different life, which you must love very much—to such a . . . well, to such a confining one as this. Do you find it awfully difficult?"

Lisbeth tried to answer the question without betraying her critical feelings toward the girls. "I get a little rattled sometimes," she admitted. "I . . . I would like to have a room by myself."

"It's hard to make a change like the one you're making," Miss Carey said thoughtfully. "Rooming with another girl is part of learning how to live. Every girl is different from every other, and doing things together can be lots of fun. There is so much to learn, Lisbeth, and so much of it is not in books."

They had reached the plebs' stairs and paused. Lisbeth wanted to talk about the flippancy that so disturbed her, but her resolution to fight things out for herself kept her silent.

"If things get too tough to chew on alone, be sure and come round to my room and talk it over, Lisbeth. Talking does help. We'll have to hurry now to get ready for lunch. Until this afternoon!" Miss Carey smiled and went on down the hall.

Lisbeth hurried up the stairs and ran down the corridor of South Hall, almost colliding with Marylin Coombs. "Oh—excuse me!" she apologized.

"That's all right," Marylin responded. "You can run in the halls if you don't get caught. There's a rule for everything, but the most important one is not to get caught."

Lisbeth slowed to a walk, not sure whether Mary-lin was serious or joking. She opened the door of her room and hurried in, leaving it ajar behind her.

A slender blonde girl, standing in front of one of the dressers, turned around to look at her. She had smooth golden skin and a petulant mouth bright with lipstick. Her eyes were very dark blue, and very angry. She was the girl who had stared at Lisbeth that day in the hotel in San Francisco. She was the girl in the squirrel coat!

Lisbeth stood, dumb with astonishment, and saw the insolent amusement that came to the girl's face as they recognized each other.

"Oh no!" she said with mock despair. "Don't tell me!"

Lisbeth could not have told her anything. She saw herself in that old coat and that wretched green hat, with her hair bushing out around it, standing gazing at the grandeur of the hotel. She felt her face turning red now, as it had then, under the mocking stare of her roommate. She groped for something to say that would be cool and courteous and still protective of her dignity. But she could think of nothing and she stood there, wilted with shock and frightened by the cool sophistication of the girl before her. Something had to be said to break this awful pause.

"You are Dorothy Clayton?" she heard her voice say. "Everybody's been asking for you. My name's Lisbeth Craig."

"I know your name," the other replied. "Lisbeth Craig, the little girl from Alaska. I've just had it drummed into me to be thoughtful about you, because you're not used to other girls. I must say a few clothes have made a difference in you."

Lisbeth turned toward her desk and put her notebook and pencil on it. The tone of superiority in the other girl's voice infuriated her. "Excuse me. They haven't changed me in the least," she replied coldly. She was rigid with anger and at the same time panicky lest she do or say something that would start a hopeless quarrel.

"Excuse *me*," Dorothy mimicked, "but if you think clothes don't make a difference, it's because you really don't know the world—or yourself either. I've just been told off on your account, and I'm in no mood to argue with you." She turned away and angrily hoisted one of her traveling bags up on the bed. "If you think St. Anne's Hall is a bed of roses, you're mistaken. I hate the place."

"I'm sorry, but if you've been told off, as you say,

it was because you were late. It had nothing to do with me." Lisbeth bristled, fighting to keep from being crushed by this overbearing girl. She realized that if she let Dorothy Clayton bully her now, her life at St. Anne's would be ruined from the start.

Dorothy turned back from her bag and looked scathingly at Lisbeth. "Are you insulting me?" she asked.

"I . . . I don't know what you mean," Lisbeth stammered, taken aback by this unfair accusation.

"Oh, so you don't know what I mean," Dorothy said, her eyes blazing. "You tell me I don't know what I'm talking about and then you look shocked when I resent it! Haven't I just put up with a half hour of Miss Townsend on the subject of my responsibility to my roommate? Nothing to do with you, indeed! I might just as well be hired out to be your keeper."

Lisbeth saw that Dorothy was beside herself with rage. Frightened and embarrassed, she did not know what to do or say. With unbearable longing, she thought of the cool blue air of Hermit Bay and the little plane at the float and Dad hugging her and whispering, "Don't let them scuttle you." Out in the hall the lunch bell chimed, but Lisbeth still stood where she was, as though she were glued to the floor.

Dorothy changed suddenly. "Come on, my little pleb," she said gaily. At the same time the door was thrust open and the girls from next door came in.

"Dot!" exclaimed Gail. "You got here at last!"

"Yes, in spite of more or less passive resistance." Dorothy smiled wryly. "The Regal T. greeted me with one of those lofty lectures about neglecting my 'dewty,' but I survived it." She finished with a sigh.

Lisbeth felt both relieved and deflated as they all went out, with Dorothy acting as though the former tense moments had never occurred. She felt as though she had had a practical joke played on her.

At the turn in the corridor they met Miss White coming out of her room. Dorothy smiled sweetly at her and took hold of Lisbeth's arm in what appeared to be a most friendly manner. "I've caught up to my little pleb at last!" she exclaimed.

"Come in for a moment, Dorothy," Miss White said, eying the lipstick Dorothy wore.

"I know what you're going to say!" Dorothy said, as she followed Miss White into the room. "I really forgot that St. Anne's is still quaint about lipstick. Oh, thanks," the girls heard her say. "It's always hard for me to remember to be a simple schoolgirl when I first come back."

She came out of the room with most of the lipstick

removed. Lisbeth had been embarrassed for her, and now she was taken aback because Dorothy herself was not in the least embarrassed. On the way to the front hall other girls, avid with curiosity, trooped along with Dorothy, slowing their pace to let Miss White get out of hearing, and then asking whether the Regal T. had really been "lofty" with her. When they reached the front hall, most of the older girls turned off to accompany the younger ones down the plebs' stairs.

Hastily Lisbeth said, "Don't leave your friends, Dorothy. I can get on alone."

"What a generous redhead you are," Dorothy replied. "All right. I'll meet you downstairs."

With relief Lisbeth turned away. She had never even imagined that there could be such studied insincerity, that a face could change from hatefulness to sweetness so completely that it made her doubt her own senses. She knew that Dorothy would make fun of her behind her back, that it would not be long before Jinny Clarke knew what she had been wearing that day in San Francisco. She went on down with Sally Reynolds, not daring to think of the months that lay ahead.

CHAPTER 9

DURING THE NEXT FEW DAYS Lisbeth tried to run at slow speed, to take her soundings, and chart her course. But Long Paul's advice, that had seemed so good when they talked in the galley of the *Vega*, simply would not work at St. Anne's. What appeared to be shoal water one day would turn out to be clear sailing the next. Dangerous reefs in these waters took many forms, and landfalls changed shape and deceived her. She longed for Hermit Bay and the sweeping southeasters of September, with the gray rain flinging its curtains across the bay and the seas carrying away the summer kelp. Here nothing seemed real. The girls seemed strange to her and she regarded them with suspicion. She felt hampered and uneasy in a world where all life seemed to ebb and flow at the chime of a bell.

Dorothy Clayton's bored and hostile attitude when they were alone made Lisbeth timid and resentful. But she kept her feelings hidden under a cloak of cool, formal manners which, in turn, seemed to irritate her roommate. As far as she knew, Dorothy had not yet told anyone of seeing her in San Francisco. But the thought of it hung over Lisbeth's head and took on an importance that was out of proportion. If they knew nothing of her life at home, they couldn't make fun of that. But if they got this one glimpse of her, as Dorothy had, they would think she came from a shabby home. She trusted none of her schoolmates, because she feared and hated the mockery and ridicule that they found amusing. On the other hand, because she had lived always among older people, she liked her teachers and trusted them. Even Miss Langley, whom she had not liked at the beginning, gained her sympathy because the girls made such cruel fun of her behind her back.

When Sunday came, the entire school went to

church in town. Lisbeth put on the dress Uncle Jim had bought her and pinned the little silver owl on the tie, thinking that it would take more than an "owlful of wisdom" to make her like St. Anne's.

"I see you shopped at Trevor's," Dorothy remarked, looking at her from across the room. "I get all my clothes there."

She was standing in front of her dresser, fastening a gold bracelet on her wrist. Her beautiful silver-and-enamel toilet set lay before her, and a picture of her father in a silver frame stood at one side. On an oval mirror tray stood three exquisite little bottles, one of them with a turquoise set in the stopper. Everything that Dorothy had was elegant and expensive.

"I liked Trevor's very much," Lisbeth said, remembering the wonderful ride downtown with Uncle Jim.

"Who wouldn't?" Dorothy inquired, putting on her suit jacket and hat. "Last year, when I was sixteen, I made Ethel promise that I'd never have to wear sweaters and skirts again. I hate them."

Dorothy always referred to her mother as Ethel and her father as Paul, a habit Lisbeth had difficulty getting used to. She had told Lisbeth that she always spent part of the summer holidays in the East with

Paul and the last part in San Francisco with Ethel. She spoke of the theater and dates with Eastern boys as though they were somehow superior to Western boys.

"I like sweaters and skirts," Lisbeth said independently. "But I like my jeans best of all."

"They're all right for ordinary kids," Dorothy replied, "but if I ever have a daughter, she'll be dressed by Trevor's, the way you are now, *all* the time."

This left Lisbeth without a reply. It was typical of Dorothy's talk, which always carried a veiled insult along with its infrequent approval. She had a reputation for extremely good taste, but it seemed to Lisbeth she merely carried on a sort of upside-down boasting by appearing to be bored with everything the others were enthusiastic about. Yet she could see that the girls were impressed. Lisbeth put on her hat and found her gloves as the bell chimed.

The little church stood on the edge of town nearest St. Anne's. It was built of redwood and had vines climbing about it and tall trees bending over it. Oleander bushes flanked the walk that led to its doors and followed another walk from the church to the rectory. At the first oleander bush the girls formed a line in pairs and entered the church in orderly fashion. People from the town were still coming in when the first chords of the processional began. In front of Lisbeth little Marty Evans was singing earnestly, and Lisbeth began to sing in spite of feeling shy because Dorothy stood silent beside her. She began to feel peaceful and comforted, and she forgot Dorothy as the little boy carrying the cross passed, followed by the choir and then finally the bishop himself.

On this first Sunday of the school year the bishop spoke especially to the girls of St. Anne's. His sermon was on kindness. He spoke of all the other qualities that are emphasized in the world today— leadership, personality, efficiency. Kindness, he told them, means more than all of these. He reminded them that they must not only remember St. Paul's words about faith, hope, and love, but must also put them first in their daily lives. Without love in their hearts their lives would be empty.

When church was over, Lisbeth walked back to St. Anne's with the others. She was inspired by the bishop's words and resolved to love her schoolmates in spite of their unaccountable behavior. She could see that the sermon had affected all of them. Jinny Clarke was quiet, and Lexy Burke walked with Sally and Betty, talking about the meaning of the bishop's words. Only Dorothy seemed out of sorts.

Jane Trenton called Lisbeth to walk with her and Anne and two other plebs. "The bishop always brings out the best in me," she declared. "Come on, Ellen. You join us too. I feel as though I could mother a dozen plebs today." Lisbeth was swept along with them, arriving at her room with a huge appetite for dinner.

Dorothy came in complaining of a headache. She lay down on her bed and asked Lisbeth to tell Miss White that she wanted to be excused from dinner. Miss White came immediately to the room.

"Are you ill?" she asked Dorothy.

"Just a headache," Dorothy said patiently.

"I don't think missing a meal will help it, do you?" Miss White said practically. "Hadn't you better eat your dinner and then come up and lie down afterwards?"

"Just as you say, Miss White," Dorothy responded.

"I can't let you stay in your room during mealtime," Miss White explained. "If you feel too badly, perhaps you had better come around to the infirmary."

"I'm not ill, really," Dorothy protested. "It's just a headache."

"I hope it will be better after dinner," Miss White said.

When she was gone Dorothy flung an arm across her eyes. "That horrid little woman!" she complained. "I can't stand her!"

"I like Miss White." Lisbeth defended her friend.

"I hardly expected you to agree," Dorothy said wearily.

"I'm sorry you have a headache," Lisbeth said. "I do hope you'll feel better soon." She went out and wandered down to the library to await the dinner bell.

As the weeks passed, Lisbeth found that in spite of her good resolutions she could not bring herself really to share life with the girls at St. Anne's. Dorothy remained superior and bored with her, and the others continued to make fun behind their backs of the teachers and some of the girls. The things they took seriously, like popular band leaders and sports, seemed trivial and even distasteful to Lisbeth. Their interest in the private lives of screen and radio stars, people whom they didn't even know, disgusted her, and she was confused by their cynicism and boredom toward classwork and school ideals. She became so blinded by their behavior as a group that she could not see them as individuals; only as "they,"

a crowd of giggling, dishonest, and sheeplike creatures, all wanting to be like everybody else. Even
with Sally Reynolds and a few others who tried to be
friendly she could not really unbend. She wanted to
be respected and liked, but along with this desire
lay a fear that she would be laughed at if she told
anyone what life at Hermit Bay was really like. She
simply could not find her bearings, so she took the
only possible part of Long Paul's advice and lay in
harbor—the harbor of study and meticulous attention to school rules and conventional manners.

Robbie had called her on the telephone and
promised to come to see her as soon as he could, but
he had not yet come. In a way Lisbeth was glad, because she could never confess to him how lonely she
was. In her letters home she described her schoolwork, her favorite teachers, and the bishop. She
could not bear to disappoint Mother and Dad by
telling them how unhappy she was, so she set her
sights on scholarship and waited. She spent her free
evenings in the library, or in one of the practice
rooms listening to Gertrude Lee play the piano.
When her roommate was visiting or listening to rec-
ords in the music room, Lisbeth took advantage of
her absence to enjoy an evening by herself.

On one such evening Miss Carey came to talk to

her. Dorothy was visiting in North Hall, and Lisbeth sat relaxed and comfortable in her bathrobe with her feet up on her bed and a drawing board on her knees. She had traced a map of the country of the Nile and transferred it to her paper. Now she was putting in the great river itself and the ancient cities. When the knock came at her door, she sighed and put her feet down.

"Come in," she called reluctantly.

The door opened and there was Miss Carey. "I'm glad to find you in, Lisbeth," she said, smiling.

Lisbeth jumped to her feet, remembering too late that she should always go to the door and open it herself. "Please come in, Miss Carey," she said. She crossed the room and closed the door and drew the upholstered chair near the window for her teacher. "I was just working on my map," she explained, feeling guilty in some unaccountable way.

Miss Carey looked at her work. "It's very good," she commented. "All of your schoolwork is of first quality." She seated herself in the proffered chair and brushed a wisp of hair back from her face.

Lisbeth retied the cord on her robe and sat down on her bed.

"I've come to ask a favor," Miss Carey said. "I need your help."

Lisbeth felt herself grow watchful and alert, as she used to feel in the forest of the Narrow Arm when she smelled a bear but couldn't see it. Miss Carey had talked to her once before about taking part in games like tennis and bowling, but Lisbeth had not responded to her suggestion. Now she smiled, knowing intuitively that her teacher realized that she expected to be drawn into some activity.

"It's got nothing to do with games," Miss Carey said. "It's much more serious, and I think you may even enjoy it, because it's a useful thing to do."

"I'm curious now," Lisbeth admitted. "What is it?"

"We need you to help with recreation for the little girls. They love to hear stories about animals, especially wild animals. I thought you might be willing to tell them some." Miss Carey looked at her earnestly.

Lisbeth liked the little girls. She had already made friends with the shy Sherman twins just by speaking to them in the halls, and Marty Evans had begged her for stories about Alaska more than once. "I . . . I would like to tell them stories," she said hesitantly, "but I'm not sure I *could.*"

"Perhaps if you think it over first and work out specific stories—like the one you told me that day we went shopping, about the mink feeding its young."

They both laughed at the reference, because Lisbeth had gone shopping only because Miss Carey urged her to, and she had had nothing to buy except the ice cream they shared together while the others were busy searching the store for trinkets. Lisbeth had seen a woman in a mink coat and had declared she would never wear a fur coat, because she knew the original owners of the fur so well. Now she began to think of the beaver and the otter and the wonderful Higgenbottom family, and she felt a longing to talk about them.

"I'll try, Miss Carey," she said. "I like the little girls." Then, feeling that her last words might give a wrong impression, she hastened to add, "I like girls like Sally and Anne too. Sally keeps trying to get me to join the riding class."

"I think you'd like it. Riding is wonderful fun," Miss Carey said enthusiastically.

"I never even saw a horse until we came to San Francisco," Lisbeth confessed. "Uncle Jim wanted me to take at least one riding lesson, but there wasn't time."

"Would your Uncle Jim like you to learn to ride?" Miss Carey asked.

"Uncle Jim wants me to do everything!" Lisbeth

told her. "When he gets back from the East, he'll come to see me. You'd love Uncle Jim. He's got red hair—and he's wonderful!"

She went on to tell Miss Carey about Robbie and Mother and Dad. She talked more than she had at any time since coming to St. Anne's Hall. She felt happy and lost track of time, so that when the bell chimed and Dorothy came in, she was taken by surprise.

"Oh, good evening, Miss Carey," Dorothy said sweetly. "How cozy you two look."

"So cozy we lost track of the time," Miss Carey responded, rising from her chair. "Shall I see you tomorrow evening then?" she asked Lisbeth.

"Yes, Miss Carey," Lisbeth assented, wishing she could keep the plan from her roommate.

"Come to my room at seven. Thank you very much." The teacher bade them both good night and left.

"What's she doing?" Dorothy asked when the door was closed. "Trying to rope you into school activities?"

"Oh, no," Lisbeth declared. "I'm going to help her out with the little girls tomorrow evening. That's all."

"They probably talked you over in faculty meeting and decided Miss Carey should do something about you," Dorothy said carelessly. "You're positively antisocial, you know."

"I don't care if they did," Lisbeth said, hating Dorothy's way of talking. "I like Miss Carey and I don't mind helping her a bit."

"I'm only trying to enlighten you." Dorothy's voice reflected her indifference. "I don't care what you do."

In spite of herself, Lisbeth did care. Her first little doubt of the sincerity of her teacher shook her confidence, but she quickly buried it. She told herself that Miss Carey was her friend as well as her adviser. She went to bed, and when the lights were out she rehearsed a story to herself about Otto, the otter who had once been her pet. She would begin with that.

CHAPTER 10

LISBETH'S SUCCESS with the little girls was outstanding as the weeks passed, and she was asked to tell the Higgenbottom story again to the whole grade school, including the young day students. She was so stimulated by this, her first success, that everything she did took on color and individuality. She found herself being included, at least by reputation, among the talented girls of the school, like Gertrude Lee and Clarissa Jones and Lexy Burke, who was wonderful at pantomime. Clarissa was St. Anne's most talented dancer and now, even with her slight training, Lisbeth sometimes worked with her. When the Thanksgiving tableau was planned, Lisbeth was given a prominent part. Now she could write home with real enthusiasm about the things she was doing with the other girls.

She had gained great popularity with the younger students, but in her own class she had been elected to no office, and she had not been included in any of the little groups the girls fell into as they became better acquainted. Instead of growing closer to the girls of South Hall, where she lived, she grew farther away from them both in attitude and interests. She lived there as people live in modern apartment buildings, without ever really knowing the neighbors she spoke to in the hall. But the love little Marty Evans showered upon her took the edge off her loneliness, and her efforts to distinguish herself in the things she could do well kept all of her hours occupied. While she was still rehearsing for the Thanksgiving tableau, she attended the meeting of the drama and dance groups to plan the Christmas pageant.

After that meeting Lisbeth came back to her room so thrilled that she burst out with talk about it. "I'm going to have a part in the ballet and understudy Clarissa Jones for the lead, besides!"

"And I'm on the committee for the Christmas party!" Dorothy responded, mimicking Lisbeth's enthusiasm. She did not even look up from the letter she was writing. "Thank heaven, I don't have to make a spectacle of myself on the stage!" she added.

Lisbeth could have bitten her tongue. "You have an odd way of looking at it," she remarked.

"Now, look here, my little cell mate," Dorothy flared up, "you may think you've become a Very Important Person, but that doesn't make me odd, as you so tactfully put it. It's not at all odd to be bored with arrangements for an hour's well-chaperoned dancing after the Christmas pageant."

"I'm sorry if I offended you," Lisbeth said, withdrawing again into herself. She had been wishing that she was an upperclassman so that she could go to the dance after the pageant, since for the young girls the party ended when the pageant was over. The holidays did not begin until the next afternoon.

"Oh, I'm not offended," Dorothy said. "That is, by you. What offends *me* is being here at all."

Lisbeth said nothing more. She hung up her skirt and sweater and put on her robe, hurrying in order to have time to read again the letters that had come from home that day. She took the enlarged snapshot of Robbie that he had sent her and stood it up against the little totem on her dresser. He was standing on the bridge of the *Vega*. The picture had been taken from the deck below, and part of the wheelhouse and the rigging showed behind and above him. Robbie looked very handsome, standing there looking down at the camera.

Dorothy looked up as she folded her letter. "Who's the handsome seafaring youth?" she asked.

"My brother Robbie—Robert," Lisbeth replied. "He's on the bridge of one of our boats."

Dorothy rose and crossed the room to look at the picture. "May I look?" she asked, picking up the photo. "He's a lot older than you, isn't he?" Her manner underwent one of those quick changes Lisbeth had grown accustomed to.

"He's six years older. He's at the University of California now."

"You're such a secretive little thing." Dorothy laughed. "Why haven't you told me you had a brother at school in this state?"

"Oh, *I* don't know," Lisbeth said, wishing Dorothy would go back to her own side of the room.

"I suppose this flatters him," her roommate remarked, putting the picture back on the dresser. "It's such a romantic pose."

"It looks exactly like him," Lisbeth answered.

"Too bad it doesn't show more of the boat. The *Vega's* our new packer."

"I should think you'd be more interested in your brother than in the boat." Dorothy laughed again and crossed the room as the eight-thirty bell rang. There was a pause; then she went on in a big-sister tone. "You keep too much to yourself, Lisbeth. A bunch of us are killing time in Betty's room tomorrow evening. Won't you join us?"

Lisbeth had begun to look at her letters. "I'm rehearsing tomorrow night," she said absently. Then it dawned upon her that this was the first time her roommate had ever suggested her spending an evening with her friends. She looked across at Dorothy, surprise showing on her face. "Thank you just the same," she said.

After lights were out Dorothy remarked, "I suppose your family will come to see the pageant. I think I'll write and ask Paul to come. Ethel's in Bermuda this winter."

"My whole family will be here and Uncle Jim besides. Afterwards, Mother and Dad and I'll fly home for the holidays and maybe Robbie and Uncle Jim, too," said Lisbeth, wondering what in the world had got into Dorothy.

But she wondered only briefly, because for the

first time since she had come to St. Anne's she was feeling content. Mother and Dad would see her in the pageant, and the next morning she would pack her suitcase and in a matter of hours they would be home, if they flew straight through without stopping. The mountains would be white all the way down to the water. The days would be short and she would come in and leave her snowshoes at the door and they would have tea by candlelight. In Alaska it would be winter, the way it ought in December, with the stars flashing in the sky above the mountaintops. She sighed happily, thinking of Hermit Bay, and sank into sleep.

The following day after gymnasium, which she still hated, Lisbeth ran around to take her shower and change. In the locker room she found Dorothy and a group of her friends deep in conversation. The girls were still in their gym suits, and Dorothy's locker was open, as though she were about to get her towel and clothes. There was always a rush for the showers, and Lisbeth opened her locker, which she never kept locked, and got her things without delay.

"We'll have to get a date for Gertrude," Leila Gordon was saying. "She doesn't seem to have any boy friends." Leila was a senior and a special friend of Dorothy's.

"It's always a nuisance trying to get dates for girls like Gertrude Lee," Dorothy said. "I can't think of anyone. My men friends all go to Eastern schools."

"I know a boy who likes music," one of the group said, "but not Gertrude's kind of music!"

Lisbeth said, "Excuse me," as she brushed past them.

"Don't rush off, Lisbeth," Dorothy said.

"I'm in a hurry," Lisbeth replied, as she made for the shower room. She did not see why it should be hard to find a partner for Gertrude, and she did not like the way they were talking about it. Gertrude was one of the nicest girls in the school, and if she did not know any boys it certainly was not her fault. Finding an empty shower stall in the steamy room, she hung her clothes on the door and then undressed inside, reaching out to put her gym clothes on another hook. Soon the water was stinging her back and she could hear only an occasional shout outside above the noise of the shower.

Why, I'll ask Gertrude if she'd like to have Robbie for a partner! Lisbeth almost spoke out loud, so pleased was she with the idea. I'll write and tell him that I can't stay up after the pageant, but he and Uncle Jim can dance for an hour. I'll ask them *both* to escort Gertrude. Then that silly committee on arrangements will change their tune. Gertrude will have the two nicest men there.

Immensely pleased with her idea, she hurried through her shower and sought out Gertrude in the practice room where she knew she would find her. Outside the door she stood still, listening to Gertrude practice. When there was a pause, she tapped on the door and entered in response to the other's call to come in.

"Excuse me, Gertrude," she explained. "I wouldn't have interrupted you, but I want to ask you something—and then I'll have to write to Robbie and I didn't want you to make other plans—that is, if you like my idea." She was suddenly embarrassed.

Gertrude laughed. "It's time I stopped anyway. But whatever are you talking about, Lisbeth?"

"About the Christmas party. You see, my brother and Uncle Jim are coming to see the pageant, and I can't stay up afterwards. So . . . well . . . I wanted to ask if they might be your partners at the dance. Robbie's nineteen and Uncle Jim isn't a bit old. He's a bachelor and awfully sweet." She felt awkward and added, "I hope you haven't asked anyone yet."

"No, I haven't," Gertrude said. "I'll be very glad

to ask your brother and Uncle Jim. The only boys I know haven't got money enough to come all the way to California just for a dance."

"My whole family is coming," Lisbeth explained, "but it's mainly to take me home for the holidays."

"You're sweet to think of me, Lisbeth. I was rather dreading the dance," Gertrude said. "I'll be happy to meet your family. It will be like going to the party with somebody I know."

They were walking down the corridor, and Lisbeth wrote Uncle Jim's and Robbie's addresses in Gertrude's notebook.

"I'll give the names to the committee and the invitations will be sent," Gertrude told her. "When you write to them, please say that I'm delighted they're coming." Before she turned into North Hall she stopped and looked at the younger girl. "I'm really awfully pleased," she said. "Thank you, Lisbeth."

Lisbeth went on to her room, feeling happy. She had just snatched Gertrude's fate from the hands of that hardhearted committee. She knew that Gertrude was a scholarship girl, and that she did not have a lot of money for clothes and things, but she was sure that Dad would admire Gertrude as much as she did herself.

At her door she met little Marty Evans, who was standing there knocking. "Oh, Lisbeth!" she cried. "I was scared I'd missed you." She clutched Lisbeth around the waist with one arm and held a tipsily printed paper in her free hand. "Will you please autograph this? It's your story about Minnie the Mink. I copied it all down, word for word."

"Of course, little blackberry," Lisbeth said. They went into the room and she sat down at the desk and wrote "by Lisbeth Craig of Hermit Bay" across the bottom of the paper.

"May I please look at the tooth again?" Marty asked.

"You're the only one in the school who appreciates that tooth. You may look at it as much as you want to," Lisbeth replied.

Marty held the bear's tooth up to her face and looked in the mirror. "Gee! It must be awful to have teeth like that in your face," she exclaimed.

"If you were a bear, you wouldn't mind," Lisbeth said. "Here you are." She handed Marty her paper and looked toward the window, noticing that the room had darkened. "Marty, it's raining!" she cried. She leaned out of the window to sniff the air. "I'm going out in it. I've been waiting and waiting for it to rain!"

"Can I go with you?" Marty asked eagerly.

"Dash around and get your raincoat. Meet me at the bottom of the stairs," Lisbeth answered.

Marty was off like a deer. A little later the two of them were walking toward the tennis courts, while the girls who had been playing were running past them, heading for the door to the gymnasium. Lisbeth and Marty walked in the rain past the courts and down the bridle path that led to the hills. They laughed and skipped and chased each other. At the gate they stopped, and Lisbeth looked at her watch.

"It's almost time for the bell!" she exclaimed. "We'll have to run all the way back if we're going to change for dinner."

When Lisbeth came panting into the room, Dorothy was just finishing dressing for dinner.

"Where *have* you been?" she asked. "Your hair's all wet."

Lisbeth began flinging off her clothes. She took her towel and rubbed her hair and face. "I've been walking in the rain," she said. "I love the rain. I thought it would never come."

She pulled her blue dress over her head and poked her feet into the shoes that went with it. The bell chimed just as she was brushing the damp curls back from her glowing face.

Dorothy looked at her, waiting for her to finish. "You really are quite spectacular, Lisbeth," she said. "You'll probably be a heartbreaker when you grow up."

"A what?" Lisbeth turned, wondering what Dorothy was getting at now.

Her roommate laughed. "You'll know in a couple of years," she said, as they started for the door. "Look," she went on, holding out her arm, "I've got a new bracelet. Rick sent it as a consolation because he can't be here for the party."

Rick was the boy Dorothy talked most about when she and her friends discussed their summer vacations. Lisbeth looked at the bracelet as they went out in the hall. It was a circle of little silver flowers, and she thought it very pretty indeed and exclaimed over it.

Dorothy took her arm and said confidentially, "If your brother wants to stay for the dance, I wouldn't mind having him for my guest. Rick hates not being able to come, but since he can't I'll be free to ask someone else."

Lisbeth was taken aback. It had never occurred to her to ask Robbie for Dorothy. She knew Dorothy did not really like her, but when she wanted to be friendly it was hard to remember how mean she was at other times. Lisbeth did not want to talk about her plans for Robbie and Uncle Jim. She drew away, feeling confused and a little embarrassed. She did not like having Dorothy hold onto her arm and she did not want to hear the laugh that she knew would come if she told Dorothy about Robbie and Gertrude.

"Oh, thank you," she murmured hesitantly. "You better not count on it. I'm . . . I . . ."

While she hesitated, trying to find words that would be just right, others girls joined them. Ellen Johnson said loudly, "I saw you out in the rain with Marty Evans," as though she were accusing Lisbeth of some misdeed. In the laughter that followed, Lisbeth replied that she liked the rain, and then she asked Dorothy to show her pretty bracelet to the other girls. As they gathered around, she edged away and went on to catch up with Sally Reynolds.

She felt that she was beginning at last to get her bearings, that she could haul anchor and move cautiously out of harbor. She felt that she was beginning to know the other girls. She knew that Dorothy was a schemer and a good person to steer clear of, because you never knew how she was going to act. She thought that if she simply avoided the subject of Robbie, Dorothy would not mention it again and a scene could be avoided. Dorothy was such a problem! But Sally was different, as was Gertrude. Lexy was different, too. She was the most independent girl in the school. Lisbeth wanted to make friends with Sally Reynolds now, but she was shy about it, not knowing just how to begin. She saw Sally and Anne Barton ahead of her and caught up with them. They glanced at her, as though expecting her to dash on past as she usually did.

She slowed down and smiled at them. "Isn't the rain wonderful?" she asked.

"It makes me homesick," Anne said. "It rains a lot where I come from."

They went on down the plebs' stairs talking about weather.

For two days Lisbeth succeeded in evading the subject of Robbie and the party. She had learned to know so well Dorothy's devious way of approaching any subject that interested her that she managed to head her off each time she began to talk about the Christmas plans. Then on the third afternoon, when she came up from practicing with Clarissa Jones, Dorothy greeted her with a sudden hostility.

"Well!" she said. "So you've gone behind my back to get Gertrude Lee to help you out with your family, as though she were your roommate. The committee had already planned to ask someone for her when here come her cards with the names of your relatives! I've never been so mortified in my life."

The suddenness of her attack left Lisbeth flustered and angry. "Don't talk to me like that," she said. "I didn't go behind anybody's back! And Gertrude can take anyone she pleases to the party. Other girls do."

"It's the little self-righteous prudes like you who do the really dishonest things," Dorothy said caustically. "I'd already told the girls that I was going to take your brother to the dance as a favor to you!"

"Why did you do that?" Lisbeth turned wide eyes upon her roommate. Her heart had begun to pound and she felt trapped and scared.

"Why did I do that?" Dorothy said furiously. "Why indeed! Don't try to be so innocent. You know as well as I that we practically had it arranged. How dared you humiliate me like this?"

Lisbeth looked at her aghast. "Why, Dorothy— you know that isn't true. We made no arrangement at all. I asked Gertrude to take Robbie and Uncle Jim that day I heard you and the others talking about her in the locker room. There was no reason to talk about it to anyone else."

"So our studious reserved little Lisbeth Craig is

an eavesdropper as well as a liar," Dorothy sneered. "I must say your innocent face fooled me, as well as everyone else. But thank goodness I know you now. My first impression of you should have told me what you really are! You'd better watch your step, Lisbeth Craig." She sailed out of the room and slammed the door behind her.

The injustice of the attack was so shocking that Lisbeth was completely nonplused. She stood staring at the door, shaken to her very bones. Never, never had she imagined that anyone would—*could*—question her honesty. Why, most of her difficulties rose from the fact that she could not compromise with honesty. If Dorothy had told her friends that she was going to the dance with Robbie, she had had no right to do so. It was her own fault, just as it was her fault that she got scolded on First Day, when she came late, and then acted as though it were Lisbeth's fault that she had got into trouble. But this was much worse. Lisbeth knew that she could not forgive Dorothy for this unless she admitted her fault and apologized.

But Dorothy did not apologize. As the days passed, Lisbeth burned under her insult until she found it almost impossible to speak to her at all.

C H A P T E R 11

LISBETH COULD NOT HAVE SAID, during the next few days, just when it was that she first became aware of a change toward her in the attitude of the girls. At first it was just a feeling. She was depressed and unhappy, because it was so dreadful to have Dorothy's words hanging over her and be unable to fight back. Her roommate had so brazenly twisted what was said into a meaning that had never been intended. How did she dare? Lisbeth's first thought was to go to Miss Carey and tell her the whole thing, but after some consideration she realized that Doro-

thy would deny everything and make it seem that
she, Lisbeth, was guilty in her own conscience.
Dorothy was clever at turning things to suit her
purposes.

On the third day after the quarrel, Lisbeth noticed that sometimes, when she approached a group
of girls, they stopped talking and she thought they
looked at her strangely. In the dining room it
seemed to her that instead of being withdrawn, as
she usually was, she was now deliberately left out of
the table conversation. When she hurried to catch
up with Sally and Anne, to walk with them, she felt
that now it was they who had grown reserved and
she who was trying to be friendly. If Dorothy were
spreading lies about her and they believed them,
then Lisbeth did not want their friendship anyway.
She stopped trying to catch them in the hall. She
ran for harbor again and gave all of her energy to
classwork and the tableau and the Christmas
pageant.

But the loneliness came back to dwell in her heart
more strongly than before, because she had begun to
taste friendliness and had found it sweet. Not only
was she lonely now; she also felt a sense of loss. She
rehearsed harder than ever with Clarissa, but Clarissa became more critical and it was not as much

fun. Lisbeth began to dread the pageant. She had written home about it in such glowing terms. Now she shrank from thinking of the day when her family would arrive and meet the cool stares of girls who were so taken in by Dorothy that they were willing to believe the worst of anyone who happened to be a victim of her anger. Dorothy was hardly ever in the room any more, except to change for dinner and to come to bed. One afternoon she complained that she could not find one of her most expensive linen handkerchiefs, as though Lisbeth were responsible for its loss.

Lisbeth turned to her and said, "Dorothy, if you are so miserable rooming with me, why don't you ask to be changed? Or should I?"

"It wouldn't surprise me if *you* did," Dorothy replied in her grand manner. "But if you think *I'm* a rat and a telltale, you're quite mistaken. I fight my own battles and I expect others to do the same."

Lisbeth was left raging and frustrated. She could say nothing that Dorothy did not turn somehow to her discredit. After that, she defended herself with silence and what confidence she could draw from her own inner being. Then one day after gymnasium the whole thing reached a climax in the place where it had started—in front of her locker next to the shower room.

Lisbeth was hurrying even more than usual, because some of Dorothy's friends were there, waiting while she got her things out of the next locker. Lisbeth made a grab for her towel and pulled it out. There was a light clinking sound on the concrete floor. She looked down, and so did Dorothy and her friends. There, by her feet, lay Dorothy's new bracelet, the circle of silver flowers Rick had sent her.

"Why . . . *there's* your bracelet, Dot!" Leila Gordon exclaimed, pointing at it with a straight arm.

There was complete silence, as all of them realized that the bracelet had fallen from Lisbeth's locker.

She stooped and picked it up, holding it out to Dorothy. "You must have put it in my locker by mistake," she said.

Dorothy made no move to take the bracelet. Her lips curled in contempt as she turned away. "You know perfectly well I never wear that bracelet in the daytime," she said. "It's been missing from my dresser for two days. After all, Lisbeth, if you're going to steal, for heaven's sake don't be so clumsy about it." She looked at her friends as Lisbeth stood there, white and speechless, holding the little silver flowers in her hand. "Come on, girls," she went on in a bored voice. "If she wants it that badly, let her keep it."

The bracelet slipped out of Lisbeth's hand without her feeling it and fell to the floor again with its silvery ring. The girls followed Dorothy toward the shower room, averting their eyes from Lisbeth as though she were a shameful sight as she stood gazing after them in despair.

Others were coming in from the gym. The mechanical clatter of keys and the slam of metal doors made Lisbeth aware of where she was. Numb with shock, she automatically got her soap and clothes out of the locker and started for her shower. As she walked between the rows of steel cabinets, her chin began to shake. Tears flooded her eyes as she rushed blindly into the shower room and made for the first empty stall she could see. She pulled off her clothes and groped for the hook to hang them on. Then she dropped the catch on the door and turned the water on full blast. In the noise of the shower she leaned against the wall and sobbed and cried aloud like a little child.

For the first time in her life she felt complete disillusionment and despair. She had looked into the face of hate, and to her horror had found that it was not ugly and self-evident as she had expected it to be. Instead, it was a smooth face, full of deception and lies. Its contempt and cruelty were only half hidden under the thin mask of customary manners. With her forehead against the clammy wall and the water beating across her back, Lisbeth cried out her hopeless agony. She had been betrayed so easily, humiliated so completely! Her face hurt with crying, and she turned away from the wall and shut her eyes and let the water fall upon her head. "I want to go home," she sobbed aloud into the roar of water. "I want to go home."

She reached out and turned off the hot water, letting the cold needles of the shower beat down upon her. They fell upon her face and her back and she hopped around under the stinging darts until finally her sobs ceased and she was gasping. She waited until she was sure she could be quiet and then turned off the water altogether. She stood there dripping and shivering. She would leave St. Anne's and never return. She would draw out all of her money and slip away and take the train North. She would find Robbie and make him send her home on a plane. In a couple of days she would be at Hermit Bay. She rubbed her hair as dry as she could, feeling a flush of joy at the thought of being home again. She would forget St. Anne's. It would be like a night-mare, queer but not scary at all once you were awake.

She became aware that the shower room was silent, the girls were all gone. She looked at the clock and discovered that she had been over an hour in the shower stall. She was still shivering and she reached for her clothes and got into them as quickly as she could. Her dream of going home was gone. She knew she could not just walk away from St. Anne's and have everybody raising a fuss about it. She shook her short hair over the heat vent and then combed it back from her face. She felt shaky and tired as she took her gym clothes back to her locker. The bracelet was not on the floor where she had left it. Someone had found it and would return it to Dorothy.

At the thought of the bracelet, Lisbeth's grief turned to anger. She was overwhelmed with help-less rage. "I don't care what they do—I don't care in the least," she told herself. "I wouldn't have all the girls of St. Anne's on a silver platter, not if they were the only living creatures on earth. They're even worse than I thought they'd be. Sheep! Just sheep! They'll all trail along with Dorothy. She'll be sweet

as honey to them and have them all feeling fright-
fully sorry for her."

She left the gym by the outside door, with her
mind racing angrily. Her chin was thrust out bel-
ligerently, and she was almost talking aloud in her
fury against the meanness and duplicity of her roommate. What had she wanted with Robbie, anyway?
She was always bragging about the men that were
clamoring for dates with her. If she had told the girls
that Robbie was her date for the party and then he
turned out not to be, it was no one's fault but her
own. But, as Lisbeth walked around the building,
she came to the realization that, no matter what the
facts of the case actually were, Dorothy intended to
ruin her.

Her anger ebbed away and a heavy feeling of fear
settled around her heart. She was aware that Dorothy had planned this, that the seeds of suspicion had
already been planted. Everyone was going to think
that Lisbeth Craig was a thief. In a sudden panic,
she stopped walking and looked about the grounds
of St. Anne's for a refuge. She wanted to flee, to
start running and keep on running until the whole
miserable experience was far behind her. But the
orderly trees and shrubbery offered no refuge. The
cries drifting to her from the tennis courts shut her

out. No one would believe that Dorothy had deliberately hidden the bracelet in her towel.

Slowly she walked on, her feet heavy on the cinder path. She was dazed and bewildered. She did not know what to do. Then she heard running feet behind her. She tried to compose her face and walk toward the side door, as though it were her intention to enter the building.

With a rush little Marty came up behind her and threw her arms around her waist. "Oh, Lisbeth!" she cried. "I've heard all about the bracelet and I know it isn't true! She's been talking about you all week! She's been doing it on purpose. She's jealous."

Lisbeth wanted to say something but she could not speak. The tears started to sting her eyes again and she fought hard to keep them back. She put her arm around Marty's shoulders and they walked on together.

"I've looked everywhere for you," the little girl said, still panting from her run. "Don't feel bad, Lisbeth. We'll catch her. Bad people always get caught."

"I can't stand it," Lisbeth whispered. "I'll have to go away. I'm going home. I'll tell Miss Townsend and she'll have to send me home." She stopped, because she was going to cry again and she must not do that. She must not let any of them see her cry, not even little Marty.

Marty was repeating, "No, no, no, Lisbeth. You mustn't give up." She hopped up and down with anxiety. "You mustn't go! We'll pray. Then we'll know what to do."

She led Lisbeth around to the outside entrance of the chapel. Hardly knowing what she was doing, Lisbeth went meekly with her little friend. They entered the chapel and knelt down together. Lisbeth gazed at the altar, not even trying to think. It was so quiet she could hear the tinkle of water in the fountain outside. The late afternoon sun came slantwise through the beautiful stained glass of the high Gothic windows, and the candles upon the white altar burned steadily in the still air. Little by little, Lisbeth felt the calm and ancient spirit of the Church comfort her. It was like the quiet of the forest on a windless day, hushed and full of wonder, needing no explanation.

"I am not guilty of any of the things she has accused me of," she whispered, gazing at the altar. "Please make her see the dreadful thing she has done, so that she can undo it."

"Oh, Lord, have mercy upon us," Marty prayed

aloud. "Make clean our hearts within us and take not thy Holy Spirit from us. Amen."

They walked out of the chapel into the hall. Then Marty clutched Lisbeth's arm. "Hang on, Lisbeth," she begged. "Don't go away. Hang on—even if it's impossible. I know you'll win out in the end!"

"Darling Marty," Lisbeth said, giving her a squeeze, "I simply should have died without you! I'll talk to Dorothy alone. She can't keep up her pretense with me alone."

They parted at the top of the stairs and Lisbeth went around to her room. Never had South Hall seemed so long. Most of the doors were open and the rooms were empty, although it must be nearly time to dress for dinner. There was a crowd in Jeanne Avers' room, and Lisbeth walked by with her face averted, remembering that Jeanne had been with Dorothy when the bracelet fell out of her towel. But as she hurried past she could not help hearing someone remark, "If she'd only confess it, it wouldn't be so bad!"

Lisbeth hurried blindly on to her room, remembering the times she had seen these same girls make cruel caricatures and cutting remarks, and then turn false smiles upon their victims.

Ellen Johnson was standing in the door of her

room, as though waiting for Lisbeth to return. "You'll catch it if anybody tells on you," she said maliciously.

Lisbeth went into her room without looking at Ellen. It was later than she had realized. She had not heard the bell, but Dorothy was already dressed for dinner. Lisbeth stopped with her back to the door and looked at her. In a tight voice that hurt as her words burst out, she said, "Dorothy, why did you do it?"

Her roommate returned her look coolly and Lisbeth saw, to her horror, that she was enjoying herself.

"Really, Lisbeth," Dorothy said, "if you're going to pretend, even to me alone, that you didn't steal my bracelet, there's nothing I can do about it. They expel girls for things like this, you know."

Lisbeth felt the blood drain from her face. They expel girls! She walked unsteadily to her bed and sat down, feeling her heart beating up in her throat.

Dorothy's expression changed to doubt. "You don't need to be so tragic about it," she said hastily. "I'm not going to report you. You've never seen *me* hobnobbing with the teachers, have you? I only ask that you keep away from me, except when we have to be in the room together."

With that she went out and closed the door behind her. Lisbeth sat where she was, too weak to move. They would send her home in disgrace! She could never prove to anyone that she was innocent. Mechanically she thought she should get ready for dinner, but she could not seem to begin. Her hands had gone cold as stones and she shivered sitting there on her bed. When the bell chimed, she felt too ill even to go and ask Miss White to excuse her from dinner. Someone knocked at the door, and she looked toward it but said nothing. Then the door opened and Lexy Graham came in and closed it.

"Aren't you coming to dinner?" she asked, trying to seem casual.

Lisbeth said nothing, and Lexy crossed the room and looked closely at her. "You look sick," she said, dropping her offhand manner. "You mustn't take it so hard. You're in a mess, but you'll work out of it in time."

Lisbeth sneezed and groped for her handkerchief. "It isn't *my* mess," she said vaguely. "It's hers."

"I'll tell Miss White you're sick," Lexy said. "You're lucky to catch a cold right now. It'll leave them with nothing to take out their spite on."

She left, and in a moment Miss White came in. "Why, Lisbeth, you do look ill," she exclaimed.

"Why didn't you tell me? I thought the other day you were looking a little pale."

"I . . . I feel awful," Lisbeth managed to say.

"You look like another flu victim," Miss White said briskly. "You get your night clothes together and come around to the infirmary. I'll run and tell Mrs. Wiley before she goes down. Can you manage by yourself?"

"Yes, thank you," Lisbeth answered. Miss White was gone like a creature of light slipping in and out of the nightmare she was trying to grope her way through. With an effort she got up and opened her closet door and stood staring into it. She should get her night clothes. She began to shiver and tears started rolling down her cheeks. All she could think was that girls were expelled for stealing, and she could never prove that she had not stolen anything. Expelled was such a dreadful word—it was the end of everything. With shaking hands she reached up and got her pajamas and her robe. If they expelled her, even Mother and Dad would never be *sure* she was not guilty. She stood there, holding her night clothes, feeling like a deserted and sinking ship.

Mrs. Wiley came in without knocking. "Goodness me, child! You do look ill," she exclaimed. "That flu strikes so suddenly!" She put a cool hand on Lisbeth's forehead. "Come," she went on, "I'll carry your things." She swept up the night clothes and got the white moccasins and Lisbeth's comb and toothbrush.

She led Lisbeth down the long, deserted corridor and to the front of the main upstairs hall. In the white infirmary there were three beds on one side and on the other two tiny rooms with a bathroom in between.

"I was just thinking that the beds wouldn't be empty long, with colds going around like they are," Mrs. Wiley said cheerfully. "But I'm afraid you've caught the real flu, from a day student probably." She turned back the white sheet on the bed in one of the little rooms. "I'll put you in here just in case," she said. "We like to keep flu isolated as much as we can."

"I can undress myself," Lisbeth said, as the house mother began hoisting her sweater up over her head as though she were one of the little girls. "Please don't miss dinner. I'm sorry I made you late."

"Oh, don't worry about that. Don't worry about a thing," Mrs. Wiley responded. "You jump into bed and relax. The maid will bring something light for you to eat."

She got a cloth and wiped Lisbeth's face when she

was in bed. "You'll be all right," she comforted. "We'll call the nurse if we need her, but I'll take care of you for now. Eat a little when your tray comes." She smiled brightly and departed for the dining room.

Lisbeth was almost asleep when the maid came with her tray. She sat up and dutifully spooned the soup into her mouth. She ate some of the fruit and then put the tray on the table beside her bed. Darkness had come down outside the window, and she snapped off the lamp on the table and lay back on her pillow.

The darkness was comforting, hiding her from the hostility she felt around her. She closed her eyes, losing herself in the darkness, until finally the shocking experiences of the day became vague and unreal in her feverish mind. She seemed to be back in her own world—in the Narrow Arm, watching a mink bring a little crab from the seaweed to eat it on the mossy rock. It was April, her last April, and the mist came streaming out of the mountains, filling the bay and covering the land until all that was left of the world was the Narrow Arm. "I will never leave you again," she told the mink. Then in the mist above her she heard the beat of wings and, without seeing them, she knew the wild swans were flying over. She began to drift out with the tide, farther and farther into the mist, and she was sad beyond words. She could never go back. She began sobbing desperately.

"Lisbeth. Lisbeth, dear! You're feverish, dear. Here, drink this."

It was Mrs. Wiley with a glass in her hand. The lamp was lit and there she was in the little white room in the infirmary of St. Anne's.

CHAPTER 12

WHEN THE NEXT DAY CAME, Lisbeth was too ill to think. She had never been ill for a day in her whole life, and now she wondered if she were going to die. She felt miserable and lonely and frightened.

After the doctor left, Mrs. Wiley came in smiling. "You're not quite sick enough to have a nurse," she said brightly, smoothing back Lisbeth's hair. "But I'm going to have my meals upstairs for a day or two, so I'll always be nearby. Sleep as much as you can, dear. Sleep is a great healer. We'll have you fit as a fiddle in a few days."

For two days Lisbeth slept most of the time. In her waking hours Mrs. Wiley hovered comfortingly about her. The school seemed vaguely distant, and Dorothy with her false accusation remained nightmarish and unreal. Then on the third day she began to rally. She could eat now, and she knew she was going to get well. Reluctantly she realized that she would have to face the school again. Sooner or later she would have to look at the faces of the girls her roommate had turned against her.

She gazed listlessly out of the window where she could see distant treetops, dry in the winter sun. Her body felt lazy and comfortable in the white bed, and she found herself dreaming instead of thinking. I must think, she kept telling herself. I must be ready. I must know what I'm going to do when I get out of the infirmary.

In the afternoon a light tap came at her open door and she looked around to find Miss Carey standing there.

"I'm so glad you're better, Lisbeth," the teacher said. "I've been feeling awfully guilty for letting you work so hard. You've worked too hard at everything."

Miss Carey looked at her with such concern that

Lisbeth hastened to say, "Oh, it's only the flu. People get it if they work hard or not, don't they?"

"I suppose they do, but just the same I've been worried about you. Look," Miss Carey went on. "Marty sent this to you. She asks about you at least six times a day." She held out a little flowerpot with real earth in it and paper forget-me-nots planted in it in a most realistic way.

"Oh, how sweet!" Lisbeth exclaimed, taking the gift. "Please thank Marty. And thank you for bringing it." She gazed at the carefully made little flowers. "There's nobody like that little Marty Evans," she murmured.

"Mrs. Wiley won't let her come to see you, for fear she'd catch the flu," Miss Carey told her. "But you'll probably be out in three more days and then Marty's anxiety will be over."

"Three days?" Lisbeth repeated. "Then I'll miss the tableau."

She spoke without enthusiasm, and Miss Carey regarded her gravely. "You're still feeling weak," she said sympathetically. "We'll miss you awfully in the tableau, but the rest and quiet will make you well enough to go on with the Christmas pageant."

Lisbeth tried to think quickly. She must say something to keep Miss Carey from suspecting that she was glad to miss the tableau. "Who's going to have my part in the tableau?" she asked, trying to seem interested.

"Why, Dorothy volunteered for it," Miss Carey answered. "She doesn't go in for things like that usually, but she wanted to do it so that you wouldn't be worried about it. She's working hard, and she'll carry it off all right."

"That's good," Lisbeth said, looking really pleased. She knew now for certain that the secret had been kept from the teachers successfully.

"Mrs. Wiley will be coming to chase me out before I tire you. I shall pop in to see how you're coming on tomorrow. Don't worry about anything," Miss Carey said, smiling.

When Miss Carey was gone, Lisbeth thought bitterly how very clever Dorothy was. She was making it appear that she felt only friendliness toward her roommate. She was so clever that she could ruin a girl's reputation and no one in authority would ever know a thing about it. She heard the rustle of Mrs. Wiley's starched white uniform and closed her eyes, pretending to be drowsing, so that she could try to figure out what she should do when the three days were up.

The next day Lisbeth was allowed to sit up in a chair. She felt so much stronger that she was able to plan how she would behave when she got out. She would be exactly as she had been when she first came to St. Anne's. If Dorothy wanted revenge, it was going to be a cold revenge. They could think what they pleased. She would avoid the other girls as much as possible. They would never suspect, when they all departed for the holidays, that St. Anne's would never see Lisbeth Craig of Hermit Bay again. She would tell the family the whole thing just as it had happened, and Dad would never think of letting her come back.

That evening immediately after dinner little Marty came panting up to the door of the infirmary. "Lisbeth!" she called in a loud whisper, tiptoeing in until she could look in at Lisbeth's door. "I ran all the way to beat Miss Wiley up."

"Marty Evans, you scoot right out of here!" Lisbeth ordered. "You'll get caught, or catch the flu!"

"I *had* to see you." Marty's big brown eyes were begging her for a moment. "I'll go, Lisbeth, but I *have* to talk to you a minute. I've told some of the girls that Dot did the whole thing herself, 'cause she's jealous of you." Marty raced on, not giving

Lisbeth a chance to interrupt. "It'll have an effect on them, you wait and see! They don't *all* believe everything Dot says."

"You're a darling, Marty, and I love you, but I'll have a relapse if you get caught in here. Do go right away," Lisbeth begged.

"All right," said Marty, backing away. "Oh, I'm so glad you're better. We'll win yet. Don't give up, Lisbeth!" She turned and scooted out into the hall, like a startled marten running for cover.

Lisbeth chuckled and then tears popped unexpectedly into her eyes. Good little Marty, sowing seeds of doubt in the ranks of the enemy. How could she desert Marty? The comfort of her decision to leave St. Anne's faded, and again she was in a quandary. How could she fight her way through, how *could* she with everything against her? She could make no decision at all as to whether she would flee or stay. She laughed forlornly, thinking of herself in a small boat trying to ride out a storm with no harbor near. Ride it out! That was it. She would try to ride it out.

On Thanksgiving Day the bishop came up to the infirmary to see her. She had been walking around, as Mrs. Wiley had instructed her to do, in order to regain her strength. When Mrs. Wiley brought the

bishop to the door, she was just returning to her little room.

"You see?" Mrs. Wiley said triumphantly. "Lisbeth is getting on splendidly."

Bishop Hastings stood in the door and talked to
her and made her laugh and feel as if she were someone extra special. Her heart lightened, and while
she talked with him she felt free of the fear that
haunted her. She wanted to tell the bishop everything that had happened. She trusted him to believe her. But Mrs. Wiley was there and she did
not know how to begin. When he had left, she stood
looking out of her window. The round bed that
had been blooming with petunias when she came to
St. Anne's was bright with poinsettias now. It
wouldn't have done anyway, she told herself, gazing
absently at the bright red of the flowers. If she told
the bishop, she knew that she would be a rat as well
as a thief in the eyes of Dorothy's friends. She could
only wait, and waiting was terrible.

In the evening, before the tableau began, Gertrude Lee came to see her, bringing a red geranium
in a pot. Mrs. Wiley let her stand at the door and
talk for a moment. Gertrude was just the same as
always, and Lisbeth realized that she did not know
what had happened. She never had much time for

visiting with the other girls, and she had no very intimate friends. Besides, Lisbeth guessed, the others would not dare gossip to a girl like Gertrude. She would never know anything about it, unless the teachers somehow found out what had happened in the locker room. Then everybody would know that Lisbeth Craig had been expelled for stealing. There would be no way for her to defend herself against Dorothy.

On Saturday Mrs. Wiley told her that she might go back to her room and her schoolwork, but she was not to exert herself for three or four days. Reluctantly she got into her clothes, and with her robe over her arm and the geranium in her hands she went back to her room. The maids had finished cleaning, but the girls were not yet back from study hall. She reported to Miss White and chatted with her for a moment, but she was only half attentive when Miss White talked about helping her make up the classwork she had missed. What happened to her studies did not seem to matter any more. There were three and a half weeks left until the Christmas holidays. She would manage to get through them somehow. What would happen then she dared not contemplate.

She put her laundry in the blue bag in her closet

and placed the geranium on her window sill. She changed into her white sweater and blue pleated skirt and was pinning Uncle Jim's little owl on her sweater when Dorothy came in from study hall. There was an awkward pause. Lisbeth wanted to speak, to seem casual and undisturbed, but she was unable to say a word. Dorothy herself seemed to have lost her accustomed poise. But only for a moment. She walked over to her dresser, saying breezily, "I hope you're feeling well again."

"Thank you," Lisbeth answered stiffly. Anger flared up in her at the sight of the other's indifferent face. Abruptly she walked out of the room and went around to the library to await the lunch bell.

It was going to be harder than she had expected. For three and a half weeks she would have to watch every word she said, would have to appear calm no matter how she felt. Already it seemed an unbearably long time. When the bell chimed, she went out into the hall and joined the stream of girls going down to the dining room. Marty came running up and walked with her. Girls from North Hall whom she did not know very well streamed by as though they had never missed her from among them, but of the South Hall girls only Jane and Sally spoke to her. She answered Jane politely, hoping she would

not shout and attract attention, but Sally was solicit-
ous and Lisbeth felt embarrassed, dreading to have
anyone feel sorry for her.

As the days went by, she made up her classwork,
but without interest and with only mediocre grades.
She became as distant and unbending as she had
been during her first weeks in the school, answering
her teachers' queries with impersonal politeness and
letting them believe that the flu had made her tired.
When Miss Carey came to talk to her, Lisbeth was
evasive and finally said she did not feel up to doing
her part in the Christmas ballet.

Miss Carey looked at her with troubled eyes. "I'll
tell you what we'll do, Lisbeth," she said. "Anne
Barton has been understudying your part on account
of your illness. We'll let her go on understudying
it, but as soon as you feel strong enough, do come
down to rehearsal again, won't you? No one else can
do it as well as you."

"I'll try," Lisbeth said. "I feel all right, just not
very energetic." She tried to laugh and be offhand
about it.

For a moment Miss Carey hesitated, regarding her
gravely. Then she asked, "Is anything wrong, Lisbeth? Anything you want to talk about?"

"Oh, no," Lisbeth said hastily, finding it hard to meet her teacher's gaze. "Nothing at all."

When the interview was over, she sighed with relief. Much as she liked Miss Carey, she *was* a teacher and she would have to do her duty if she got wind of trouble among the girls. There was no one she could talk to, no one at all except little Marty, and she was in constant fear lest Marty make a slip of the tongue and let the secret out.

After church on the following Sunday, Lisbeth hurried to her room to remove her coat and hat, so that she could rush around to the library in order to avoid Dorothy. As she came in, she thought she saw the flounced side of her bedcover move. Then she distinctly heard someone panting. She drew the cover up and looked under the bed. There, lying on her stomach, she saw Marty, still wearing the coat and little red cap she had worn to church. Marty had run so fast she was still gasping, and she stared back at Lisbeth quite unable to talk.

"Marty Evans, come out from under my bed," Lisbeth commanded. "You'll get into trouble! Please do. Please, Marty," she finished desperately.

Marty made frantic gestures with one arm. "Cover me up, Lisbeth," she gasped. "Quick, before she comes! Detectives have to watch people if they want to find out anything. Oh, please, Lisbeth, before she comes."

There were voices outside the door and Lisbeth dropped the flounce, not knowing what else to do. She heard Dorothy's voice. "Of course she got away with it. Her type always does. But it's such a bore to have to watch things all the time. I'd rather ignore the whole business."

"Well, I wouldn't leave anything of value lying around, if I were you," Jinny Clarke's nasal voice responded.

They were talking about her, talking in that awful way. As the door opened, Lisbeth busily put her hat and coat in her closet, pretending she had not heard. There was a group outside, and now Gail Hathaway said, "Well, see you later," and moved on. Dorothy came into the room, saying, "Wait, Jinny. I'll get you that list." Then she saw Lisbeth and said, "Oh, hello," as she crossed to her desk.

Lisbeth was confused and angry. "I'm just going to the library," she replied irrelevantly. She hurried out past Jinny Clarke without even looking at her. Her face was burning as she walked along the hall to the top of St. George's Hill, where the library door stood open. The room was empty, and she went to the periodical table and sat with her back to the door, staring at an open magazine. How dared Dorothy keep on with this dreadful talk? Could it be possible that she wanted to make it embarrassing for Lisbeth to allow Robbie and Uncle Jim to come to the dance at all? She stared blindly at the pages before her until the dinner bell chimed.

In the dining room Sally and Lisbeth and Anne were all at Miss Langley's table again, as they had been at their first dinner in the school. In the meantime they had rotated around the entire dining room, assigned to a new table with different girls each week, and now they were back together where they had started. Lisbeth was still so outraged by what she had overheard at her door that she could not bear to look at Jinny sitting across from her. She was worried over having left Marty under her bed, and she kept trying to look at the little girls' table at the far end of the room. She did not see Marty and she became wholly preoccupied with thoughts of her. When she felt Sally give her a little poke under the table, she realized that Miss Langley had spoken to her.

"Oh, I beg your pardon, Miss Langley. I'm sorry. I didn't hear you." Angrily she felt herself blushing.

"You're too young to be growing absent-minded," Miss Langley replied, her earrings quivering as she laughed. "I was asking about winter," she went on. "We see so little of it here. I was asking about your Alaskan winter."

Lisbeth tried to say something about the winter at Hermit Bay, but she was thinking that Dorothy had not come into the dining room. Neither the bishop nor Miss Townsend was at the center table. Lisbeth was filled with anxiety as she tried to listen to and answer questions about the winter at Hermit Bay. Just as the soup plates were being taken out, Marty came into the dining room with Miss White. It was so unusual for anyone to come late to the dining room that there was a pause in the murmur of conversation, as the girls turned their heads to look. Marty looked solemn and important as she marched to the faculty table, made her apologies, and then proceeded to her own chair. Under the expert guidance of the teachers, table conversations picked up where they had left off and the murmur filled the room again.

"Listening to wolves howl on a snowy night sounds very frightening," Miss Langley said.

Lisbeth's heart had begun pounding. They had caught little Marty! "Yes," she replied, "I mean, no —the wolves sound wonderful in winter when they're running."

"I'm sure you love them," Jinny said from across the table, and everyone laughed.

After that, Lisbeth tried to concentrate on the conversation. To cover her anxiety, she found herself talking about Hermit Bay, about how a marten looked on the snow, and about the places where the bears slept through the winter. To her surprise, she suddenly realized that the girls were all listening, even Jinny Clarke. She felt almost hysterical, thinking that by evening she would be on trial before Miss Townsend, with no way to explain Marty except by telling the truth, and then no way to defend herself except by appealing to Dorothy, who she knew would have no mercy.

When the meal finally ended, she had to go out into the hall with her own group, because it was against the rules for the girls to crowd the anteroom by waiting for each other there. Marty's table would come out last, since it was farthest from the door. When she got into the hall, Lisbeth tried to slow down so that Marty might catch up, but she found Miss White waiting for her.

"Lisbeth," the teacher said, drawing her aside, "Miss Townsend would like to see you in her study."

Lisbeth was stunned. She had not expected it so soon. She was not prepared. Mechanically she said,

"Thank you, Miss White." Her knees felt as though they would never carry her around to the front hall. To avoid talking, she hurried away from Miss White. She could not talk. Her tongue was stiff in her mouth. She kept trying to swallow, because her mouth was dry. She kept on trying as she reached the front hall. She would have to say *something* in Miss Townsend's study.

CHAPTER 13

FROM HIS GOLDEN FRAME on the landing St. George gazed serenely down upon the girls, as they crossed the front hall of St. Anne's. Lisbeth walked alone toward Miss Townsend's door near the foot of the stairs. The upperclassmen and teachers began slowly mounting the wide stairway, while the younger girls, in pairs and in groups, went on to the north corridor. Giggles were suppressed and voices kept low, but as always there was an air of expectancy, as though they were making plans that would burst into action as soon as they reached the upper hall.

Lisbeth saw them as in a dream, their smiling faces, their absorption in one another, their glances darting back, as they slowed their pace to wait for a friend. They were bound together by a bond that excluded their elders, as a secret society excludes the uninitiated. Lisbeth was the only one walking alone, and she became conscious of her aloneness and was frightened. She had always thought of herself as self-sufficient, but now she felt herself to be an outcast. She seemed to see her life at St. Anne's in terms of the things she wished she had done. She remembered those bright days when she had worked so happily on her part for the pageant, when she had almost reached the point where she could learn to be friends with Sally and Anne and Clarissa. She remembered how she had always drawn back, as though waiting for the others to show proof of their sincerity, as though no such proof were required of her. She wished with all her heart that she had a friend of her own age who would understand exactly how she felt.

But it was too late, too late for tears, too late for anything. She lifted her hand and knocked upon the dark panel of the door. She heard Miss Townsend's voice ask her to come in. Her hand felt numb on the cold bronze knob, as the wide door swung open and she stood hesitantly on the threshold. A fire burned comfortably in a little grate. Shaded lamps filled the room with a mellow light, and there was a familiar fragrance in the air. To the left, heavy wine-colored drapes were drawn across the windows. Miss Townsend sat at her desk. With a feeling of faintness Lisbeth realized that Dorothy Clayton was also in the room. She was sitting on a straight chair staring at the opposite wall. She did not even look around as Lisbeth came in.

"Come in, Lisbeth," Miss Townsend said again. "Come and sit here." She indicated a chair on the other side of her desk.

Feeling like one condemned, Lisbeth tried to say, "Thank you," as she crossed the room. The words came out in a hoarse whisper and she was embarrassed, not because of Miss Townsend, but because of Dorothy Clayton. She would never let Dorothy see her break, never. Not if she had to bite her tongue to make it talk. She straightened her shoulders and repeated, "Thank you," clearly, as she walked to the chair. Then she saw that there was a coat lying upon the desk, her own coat, and beside it was one of the exquisite little bottles from Dot's dresser, the one with the turquoise stopper. It was the scent from the bottle that she smelled. She sat down on the edge of the chair, feeling completely bewildered as she clasped her hands together to stop their trembling.

Miss Townsend looked at her with such kindness and understanding in her eyes that Lisbeth felt herself melting. She had to make an effort to keep her lips from quivering.

"We find ourselves in a very difficult situation, Lisbeth," Miss Townsend began. "I am hoping that with honesty and kindness we can solve it." She looked appealingly at Dorothy, who continued to stare coldly at the wall. Miss Townsend's face was troubled and she paused before going on. "It is so easy to say a thing that can never be taken back, so easy to do a thing that can never be undone," she continued. "But, fortunately, this can be undone. It is not too late for restitution." She turned from Dorothy and looked into Lisbeth's eyes. "A great injustice has been done you, Lisbeth. We know you must have suffered . . . dreadfully."

Lisbeth could not believe her ears. "You . . . you *know?*" she said, almost in a whisper.

"I know that you have been falsely accused," Miss Townsend answered, her own voice trembling as she spoke. "Falsely accused of theft, which is a dreadful thing. I know you have borne it with fortitude and courage. I regret, deeply regret, that such an experience was yours at St. Anne's."

Lisbeth turned to look with amazement at her roommate's face. She did not yet understand all that had taken place, but she felt an undeniable flood of gratitude run through her, warming her hands and making her dizzy with relief. "I know you don't like me, Dorothy," she burst out. "But thank you for telling Miss Townsend the truth. Oh, thank you!"

Miss Townsend looked down at her desk. Dorothy continued to stare into space, as the silence stretched between them until Lisbeth knew it must explode unless something was said. With a shock she realized that Dorothy had not confessed, that she had been found out. She was trying to appear bored and indifferent.

"Perhaps," Miss Townsend said, rising from her chair, "perhaps if I leave you to talk it over, you may work it out together."

Both girls stood up as she moved out around the desk. "Remember that kindness is greater than pride." She put her hand gently on Dorothy's shoulder in a most appealing gesture.

Dorothy drew away as though her shoulder had been burned. "I won't talk to her," she said.

"There's no need to leave us alone, Miss Townsend. I won't stay here. I said I would leave St. Anne's immediately, and I will."

Her voice was so harsh that Lisbeth shuddered. She remembered her feeling of hopelessness when she herself had sworn to leave St. Anne's.

"I don't know what more you could ask than for me to leave!" Dorothy went on. "I hate it here. I *want* to leave." Not once had she looked at Lisbeth.

"As I have tried to tell you, there is a great deal more to do than to run away," Miss Townsend said patiently. "You are upset now. You cannot mean what you say. You need time to think."

Dorothy stood, white and trembling with anger, as Miss Townsend took up the telephone on her desk and pressed a button on a little box. "Mrs. Wiley, will you please come to my study?" she said. "Thank you."

She turned to Dorothy, who was again staring rudely across the room. "We'll say nothing more now," Miss Townsend said firmly. "Mrs. Wiley will give you a room in the infirmary for the present, Dorothy. Please try to think this out. We'll talk again tomorrow."

Dorothy went with Mrs. Wiley without a word, like a prisoner. Lisbeth stood where she was, remembering her own trip to the infirmary, her own misery and wretchedness. She was so glad to be exonerated that there was no room for bitterness toward Dorothy. She yearned only to put the whole thing out of mind as one forgets a nightmare.

"Please sit down, Lisbeth, over here." Miss Townsend indicated a chair near the fire. "I think I should tell you how this discovery came about," she said. "There will be talk, of course. All we can hope is that it will be short-lived."

Lisbeth nodded, looking gravely at Miss Townsend's tired face.

"Your little friend, Marty Evans, discovered your roommate hiding her expensive perfume bottle in your coat pocket. Marty was playing detective." She smiled, and then the shadow crossed her face again. "I wish, with all my heart, that Dorothy would confess her fault. I know that you would forgive her."

Lisbeth nodded vigorously. "I already have," she declared. "I'm so relieved to have it over. Little Marty! That dear little Marty!" She looked at Miss Townsend with brimming eyes, and then she blushed, because she wanted to keep calm and not complicate matters any more.

"Tears are natural," Miss Townsend said gently. "Don't feel embarrassed." Then she went on.

"When Marty thought Dorothy had left the room, she came out of hiding only to find that she was still there—merely out of her view. Little Marty clutched your coat in her arms and fled down the hall as fast as she could go, with Dorothy in pursuit."

Lisbeth wiped the tears from her eyes as she listened to this description of Marty, so desperately bent upon saving her.

"She had the good fortune to run squarely into Miss White just as Dorothy was about to catch her," Miss Townsend continued. "Miss White called them both into her room and heard Marty's story. Marty showed her your coat with the perfume bottle in the pocket and poured out the whole story right from the beginning."

Miss Townsend paused and sighed. "Dorothy insisted she was only hazing you, but she admitted placing the bracelet and the bottle among your things. If you can tell me why she did it, Lisbeth, it may help us to make her understand that she must not run away from her responsibility, but face it and clear you publicly."

Hesitantly, Lisbeth told her the story of the dates for the party, of her overhearing the girls in the locker room, and asking Robbie and Uncle Jim for Gertrude. "I didn't think Dorothy would . . . would just assume that I was going to ask them for her," she explained. "But she did . . . and she . . . she told everybody that she was asking Robbie as a favor to me." Lisbeth blushed, feeling uncertain whether or not she should tell this at all, but not knowing how to avoid it. "What I did made her angry. I can see now how it embarrassed her," she added. "I should have made it clear to her right away. I'm so sorry I didn't."

"I understand," Miss Townsend said. "Thank you, Lisbeth, for being so honest about it. I know there is a good deal more that you are too kind to tell. We shall try to make Dorothy understand that you had no intention of hurting her. I hope we shall be able to make her see that she must acknowledge what she has done and atone for it."

She stood up and Lisbeth got quickly to her feet. As they parted, Miss Townsend told Lisbeth that she hoped St. Anne's could make up for the unhappiness she had suffered. Lisbeth felt light as a feather and at the same time a little awestruck as she walked around to the plebs' stairs. She felt that she was seeing St. Anne's for the first time. She could face the girls now without fear. She could work in the pageant and write home about it. She might even take riding lessons, as Sally had once urged her to do. In the dim light of the plebs' stairs she saw Marty's little figure spring up from the bottom step.

"Oh, Lisbeth! You're here at last!" Marty cried. "I've been waiting ever so long."

They hugged each other, and Lisbeth tried to tell Marty how grateful she was. "You saved me, Marty," she ended finally, as they went up the stairs. "I don't see how you did it all alone!"

"If Miss White hadn't come out when she did, Dot would have got the coat back. She would have, in just another second," Marty told her excitedly. "But I saw her do it! She couldn't deny that. I told the whole thing to Miss White, and then we had to go over it all again in Miss Townsend's room. Miss White remembered the day you got so sick and I told her why. Dot tried to pretend she was only hazing you all along and would have told everybody in time, but I just know they saw through that!"

"Poor Dot," Lisbeth said. "She's made it worse and worse for herself. If she could only say she did it and is sorry, it would be over with."

"Poor Dot," Marty exclaimed in astonishment. "Why, Lisbeth, she nearly killed you! She deserves what she's getting."

"But it's over now, Marty," Lisbeth insisted.

"Let's not talk any more than we have to about it."

"Everybody's talking about it," Marty answered in a tone of satisfaction. "They're mostly furious at Dot. After rest period they'll decide what they're going to say to you."

"After rest period! Marty, I forgot what time it is!" Lisbeth exclaimed. "Why aren't you in your room like everybody else?"

"I *had* to see you, Lisbeth," Marty explained. "I'll slip back now and nobody'll know."

Lisbeth started down South Hall, but before she reached her room the bell chimed for the end of rest period. Doors opened and the girls came out, many of them still in their bathrobes. Lisbeth remembered the discomfort of First Day, when she had met them here in this hall. As they looked at her now, she smiled, trying to think of something appropriate to say. She was wishing one of them would speak first when Jane Trenton sprang out and grabbed her by the shoulders.

"Lisbeth Craig!" she exclaimed. "Why didn't you tell us what Dot was doing?" She gave Lisbeth a rough, friendly shake. Betty and Jeanne, Anne and Sally came out of their rooms and stood nearby. "Don't you ever suffer in silence again," Jane lectured. "It'll interrupt your growth!"

In the laughter that followed others gathered around them, some uneasy in their manner and some openly sympathetic.

"Dot certainly pulled a rough one on you," Betty Gray declared, towering over Lisbeth.

"You've got plenty to hold against us too," Jane said, "but you must remember you've never given us a chance to know you."

Lisbeth blushed, as she started to explain to Jane that she had not meant to be unfriendly. Jeanne Avers interrupted. "Tell us about the Regal T.," she said. "What did she say to Dot?"

But Jane Trenton understood that Lisbeth did not want to discuss it. "School always starts off with some people misunderstanding other people. I hereby declare a truce in South Hall!" she shouted with a wide sweep of her arms.

Above the chatter of assent Jeanne Avers spoke again. "Tell us what happened in the Regal T.'s room," she insisted.

Lisbeth looked squarely at Jeanne, remembering that she was one of Dorothy's best friends. "Miss Townsend was wonderful," she said.

There was an awkward pause. Then someone asked, "Where's Dot?"

Lisbeth felt all eyes upon her as she answered hesitantly, "She has a . . . a headache. She's with Mrs. Wiley." Confused, but feeling that now was the time to say the right thing, she added, "She needs her friends now."

"She's no friend of mine," Jeanne said quickly. "She's made fools of all of us."

Again there was an embarrassed silence. This time Sally Reynolds spoke up. "If Lisbeth can forgive her, you certainly ought."

This comment started them all talking at once, and no one saw Miss White coming toward them from the turn in the hall.

"Girls! Girls!" Miss White's crisp voice brought silence in its wake. "Girls, please do not loiter in the hall in your bathrobes." The group had already begun to drift apart when she came up to Lisbeth and Jane. "Please let us have as little talk as possible about what has happened," she advised. "If you must talk, try to be charitable," she finished, looking at Jeanne Avers.

The group broke up in silence, even Jane Trenton being without words for once.

It was a tremendous day in Lisbeth's life. In the evening she talked with Miss Carey and with Gertrude Lee, who wept because she had not realized that Lisbeth had been in need of a friend. When

Miss White bade her good night, she said, "Keep steady, Lisbeth. Learn from this, and don't let what has happened make you bitter."

Lisbeth went to sleep knowing that her life was changing, feeling that she was on the brink of great discoveries.

CHAPTER 14

THE NEXT MORNING Lisbeth woke up feeling both elated and anxious. This was the day when she was to be exonerated before the whole school. After to-day everything would be changed again. Miss Carey had told her that the bishop himself would talk to her today. He was going to talk to Dorothy, too. By night everything would be straightened out and then . . . why, then, Lizbeth thought, I can set my course and start sailing. She resolved to begin being friendly today, even though after today it would be easier.

As she stepped out of her room to go to chapel, Louise and Ellen came from their room across the hall.

"Good morning!" Lisbeth said, smiling at them. Then she found herself blushing with the suddenness of her greeting.

Ellen stared at her in surprise, and just then Gail and Georgia came into the hall and joined the group.

Lisbeth stood there, smiling into Ellen's astonished eyes.

"I knew all along you didn't do it, because you couldn't have," Ellen declared in her abrupt manner.

The others laughed. "That was right penetrating of you, Ellen," Louise said teasingly.

There was an uncomfortable pause that ended when Gail Hathaway said, "We're all going to be late to chapel if we don't get moving." She spoke casually, as if nothing unusual were happening.

Lisbeth went ahead with the younger girls, wishing she could be as poised as Gail. She tried to seem calm, but each time she said good morning, and the girls gathered around, she nearly melted with shyness no matter how hard she tried not to.

After chapel when they were on their way to

breakfast, Sally and Lisbeth and Anne had a brief, earnest talk with Lisbeth. Sally and Anne were apologetic because they had not been able to defend Lisbeth when she needed them. In her turn, Lisbeth was regretful that she had never given them a chance to be friends with her. Lisbeth confided to them that she was to talk with the bishop in his office after classes were over. They sympathized with her anxiety and understood her wish to get it all over with. Lisbeth experienced the sweetness of companionship, the understanding of friends who knew exactly how one felt about things. All day she was stirred by feelings she never had known she possessed. She loved Sally and Anne and Miss Carey and little Marty—and St. Anne's, with a love that kept expanding to include more and more as the day passed.

When the last class ended, Lisbeth closed her algebra book and watched the monitors erasing equations from the blackboard. Ellen Johnson was one of them. As she rubbed in energetic little circles on the board, her body wiggled and her pigtails swung back and forth. Lisbeth smiled as she watched. She had never noticed before how much like one of the little girls Ellen was. She did not look any older than Marty from the back. Georgia Marsden followed her glance, and in a moment the whole class was enjoying Ellen's busy back. A giggle rippled over the room. Miss White looked up from her papers and the girls at the board turned to see what had happened. Lisbeth blushed as several pairs of eyes turned toward her.

She looked at Miss White. "I . . . I started it," she said. "I thought Ellen looked so cute from the back. I couldn't help smiling."

"Ellen is a vigorous worker and I'm sure she doesn't mind being appreciated," Miss White answered.

"You wiggled your pigtails," Anne Barton said to Ellen.

The whole room, including Ellen, burst into laughter. For the first time Lisbeth found herself part of one of those sudden bursts that she had found so irritating when she first came to school. Now, like the others, she was trying to suppress her giggles as they left the room.

On the way to study hall, Lexy Graham and two other sophomores from North Hall joined Lisbeth and her friends.

"Did you hear that Dot Clayton's father came this morning?" Lexy asked.

"No, I hadn't heard," Lisbeth replied, feeling anxiety like a sudden cold hand on her heart.

"Yes," Lexy went on, "he's here. He came by plane, so Jinny tells me. She saw them in the front hall." There was a pause while they all looked thoughtful. "That means," Lexy went on, "that Dot's being so obstinate the Regal T. can't handle her."

"I heard she wouldn't even *apologize* to you," one of the others said, looking questioningly at Lisbeth.

Lisbeth tried to answer, feeling suddenly embarrassed again and fearful of the difficulties that still lay ahead. "I guess she needs time to think," she said anxiously.

It had seemed such a simple thing for Dorothy to make a clean breast of it and start anew, but this news of her father's coming made everything more complicated. Lisbeth hoped apprehensively that there would not be another scene like the one in Miss Townsend's room.

They had reached the study-hall door, and Lexy put a hand on her arm. "Don't lean over backwards to make it easy for Dot," she advised. "She's older than you."

"Maybe when the bishop talks to her she'll feel different," Lisbeth said.

"She'll be dramatic to the end," Lexy replied wisely. "Don't expect her to change."

Miss Carey was study teacher for the period. As Lisbeth entered the long room, she beckoned her to come to the desk. "The bishop wants you in his office now," she told her quietly. "After today you can put the whole thing out of your mind—except what you've learned from it," she added, giving Lisbeth a comforting smile.

As she went toward the bishop's office, Lisbeth remembered her first day at St. Anne's, when she had looked at the bronze plate on the bishop's door. It seemed a very long time ago, so long ago that she must have been only a child then. She paused before the door for a moment and then knocked lightly on it. She became aware that across the hall a man was pacing to and fro in the reception room. That must be Dorothy's father. She glanced up nervously as the door opened. The bishop stood there looking down at her with his keen, compassionate eyes.

"Come in, Lisbeth," he said. He put his arm around her shoulders and led her into the room.

There, facing them, was Dorothy, sitting rigidly in one of the deep leather chairs. Her face still wore the hard resentful look that Lisbeth had grown to know so well.

"Dorothy," the bishop said, "come here."

Dorothy rose and moved reluctantly toward them.

"There has been enough talk," he told her, putting his other arm around her shoulders. "Now I want you to look at Lisbeth Craig. Let the pride go out of your heart, child. You can see that Lisbeth has no bitterness in hers."

Dorothy did not look at Lisbeth. With her face set in an expression of stubbornness she looked past her.

"It isn't so hard to say, 'I'm sorry,' is it?" Bishop Hastings coaxed gently.

"For your sake I'll try, Bishop Hastings," Dorothy answered, staring at Lisbeth coldly.

With a gesture of helplessness Bishop Hastings dropped his arms. "Not for *my* sake," he said. "It's for your own sake, my child." His voice showed such distress that Lisbeth, watching her roommate remain unmoved, looked down at the floor in shame. She wanted desperately to say something, but she could only stand and wait.

"You must not evade your responsibility," the bishop continued patiently. "You will suffer all your life if you do. It is for your own sake that I ask you to cast the pride out of your heart, that good may abide there."

Dorothy stared out of the window in silence.

After a pause the bishop turned to Lisbeth. "I

shall exonerate you before the student body, Lisbeth, since your accuser has refused to do so herself. Your innocence must be understood, not indirectly through gossip, but openly and honorably." Standing before Dorothy, he continued, "The door is not closed to you, my child. I shall continue to pray that you will come to understand your wrong and confess it with an open heart."

As they left the bishop's office, Dorothy went straight across the hall to the reception room, as though Lisbeth and the bishop were not there at all. Lisbeth felt a sudden flash of anger. How could Dot behave so rudely to Bishop Hastings! She felt his hand on her shoulder as he walked a little way down the hall with her.

The Bishop looked down at her flushed face. "Thank you, Lisbeth," he said, smiling. "You have done all that you can do. Keep your heart free from anger, child. It will not be difficult if you remember that Dorothy has had no loving home to grow in, as you have. God bless you."

Before she could reply, he had turned to go back to Mr. Clayton and Dorothy. Lisbeth could only look after him, as her anger died out. Moved almost to tears, she went on to study hall.

Before study hall ended, it was announced that

the girls were to come to chapel at the sound of the closing bell. Lisbeth sat, tense and preoccupied. Now that everything was changing, she seemed to see the full stretch of time from that dreadful day when Dorothy's bracelet fell out of her towel, to the time ahead when the bishop would restore her dignity to her. It was hard to remember her own agony of the past weeks, now that it was gone. She was aware that a few of the girls had never believed her guilty, that many of them had been indifferent, and that some had supported Dorothy in her accusation. If only Dot would make a clean breast of it, the whole thing would be forgotten in a few weeks. She had learned that no matter how excited the girls might be, most of them soon forgot what it was that had moved them. There was already a rumor that Dot was to be expelled, but Lisbeth knew that this could not be true. If Dot left St. Anne's, it would be because she would not admit her fault. When the bell rang and they left the classroom, the hall was buzzing with talk.

Lisbeth walked between Sally and Anne. Without any words, they seemed to sense her nervousness and her unwillingness to talk about Dorothy. The rest of the freshman class came along behind them, and Lisbeth felt protected as she never had before. It was like having her own strength multiplied. She felt safe from the curious glances and the gossip and speculation of the girls she knew less well. When they entered the chapel, the little girls were already seated in front. Miss Townsend and many of the teachers were in their pews. Lisbeth glanced quickly around, hoping to see Dot and her father, but they were not there. As the last of the girls entered the chapel and seated themselves, she could feel the tenseness of their waiting.

When the bishop entered, they all rose to their feet. His face was grave, and the lines on either side of his mouth seemed to have deepened as he turned to face them in the silence. He looked at them all standing there before him, and then he began the Lord's Prayer and they all knelt and said it with him.

When the prayer was over and they were seated, he spoke to them.

"One of our number has suffered the pain of false accusation. Most of us were guilty of participation in this persecution of her, either actively or by indifference. So I have called you all here that we may confess our fault and put our hearts right with God and with each other. To be falsely accused is a shocking thing. Lisbeth Craig has suffered this false accusation and she has borne her suffering with courage and fortitude . . . and with charity toward her accuser.

"Let us realize that Lisbeth Craig has come through this experience with her colors flying. Many of us have not. She was tempted to flee and did not; she was confused and waited to find the answer in her own heart; she suffered and yet harbored no bitterness."

Lisbeth's eyes had never left the bishop's face. Now suddenly they filled with tears and his image grew misty, until the tears overflowed and dropped down upon the prayer book she held in her hands. She heard his deep voice fill with emotion as he went on.

"All of us here at St. Anne's are a part of this experience that Lisbeth Craig has borne so well. Let each one search her heart, as I have searched mine, to find how much responsibility is hers. Let each one ask herself these questions: Did I accept too eagerly the condemnation of another? Was I indifferent to the suffering of another? Have I grown so careless and self-absorbed that I no longer notice an unhappy face or a schoolmate standing lonely and apart?"

After each one of these questions the bishop

waited, as though giving each girl time to answer to herself.

"Indifference is the worst of all our faults," he said softly, "because it tempts us to deceive ourselves, to say that because we did not notice we were not guilty. Let each one be alert to the dangers that may destroy us through indifference, carelessness, or self-deception. Let each one have the courage to accept full responsibility for her own attitude even though she did nothing.

"Out of your hearts will come the truth if you but heed it.

"Every experience is something added to our lives. When we err, let us not waste the experience. Let us learn the lesson that it teaches. St. Anne's will always open its doors with joy for the return of the lamb that has strayed."

The bishop paused as though waiting for Dorothy to come in, but she did not come and there was no sound in the chapel. After a moment he said the familiar words, "Let us pray," and they all knelt while he read the prayers.

After he had blessed them and left the chapel, the girls went out quietly into the hall. There was little talk among them. Those who were near Lisbeth spoke to her in subdued voices and with a shyness she had not seen before. There was an air of solemnity upon them, as though the bishop's words about the shocking behavior of their schoolmate had left them amazed and somehow chastened. Lisbeth walked with Anne and Sally, feeling for the first time the meaning of the ideals of St. Anne's.

When they reached South Hall, there were no gossiping groups in the corridor. The girls, going quietly to their rooms, wore a thoughtful air. Lisbeth left her friends at their doors and went on to her room, still not quite believing that Dorothy had left St. Anne's. She opened the door and went in. Dorothy's side of the room was empty. The dresser top was as smooth and unadorned as it had been on First Day, and her open closet door showed only a row of hangers.

Ellen Johnson came from across the hall and stood looking into the room. "I guess the bishop expelled her all right," she said flatly.

"No, he didn't," Lisbeth protested. "He couldn't have! Didn't you listen to what he said? He said St. Anne's would open its doors with joy. . . ."

"Oh, I heard that," Ellen interrupted. "Probably he didn't really expel her, but it amounts to the same thing. She won't ever repent. She's the wrong type."

Jane Trenton, Louise, Betty Gray, and Gail had come in while Ellen was talking. "For heaven's sake, Ellen," Louise said, "didn't you understand anything Bishop Hastings said?"

"Dot Clayton's gone," Ellen announced, ignoring the question.

Jane looked at the empty half of the room. "She doesn't know what she's doing," she said. Then with characteristic directness she went on. "We're all sorry, Lisbeth. South Hall is ashamed of itself. Please believe us and ask us in."

"Oh, excuse me," Lisbeth cried. "Come in," she invited them, laughing because the girls were already in the room. She pulled forward her chair and the one on the other side of the room. "Please sit down, everybody."

There was a pause and she knew she must answer Jane's apology. "Thank you, Jane." She looked at the four older girls. "Thank you all for coming in," she said, trying to keep her voice from showing the emotion she felt.

"We'd never have believed Dorothy if we had known you better, Lisbeth," Betty said in a very grave tone. "You never gave us a chance to get acquainted with you, you know."

"I realize that now," Lisbeth said quickly. "I . . .

I didn't know how to make friends," she added, embarrassed by the other's gravity.

Jane sprang up and hugged her. "We must have seemed a queer lot to you at first," she said. "Let's not make speeches, Betty!" she added.

"Jane'd make a good house mother," Ellen observed, still standing in the doorway.

"At last I've found my calling!" Jane let out one of her hearty shouts of laughter.

Lisbeth laughed with Jane, just for the fun of laughing. She asked Ellen to come and sit on her bed. Soon others, hearing the laughter, were at her door. Her room was filled with girls greeting her as though she had just got back from a journey. But shyness could not last long with Jane Trenton in the room and soon they were all talking about the coming holidays.

That evening Miss Carey called a meeting of the pageant committee. There was little time left and still a great deal to do. Now that the undercurrent of bad feeling was gone, the girls worked enthusiastically on the plans, filling in every minute of time remaining before vacation should begin. Lisbeth entered into the planning shyly at first, but soon recaptured the feeling of excitement she had first had when she began working on the ballet.

As the days passed, the school was teeming with eagerness and anticipation. Lisbeth worked on her solo dance in the snowflake ballet and, with Anne, she sang in the angels' chorus of little girls to help keep them on pitch. She was completely enchanted with the pageant as the time came for the group rehearsals. It seemed to her to be flawless, with Gertrude's magnificent piano playing, the older girls' chorus, the scenery painted by the art class, and Miss Carey's directing, which gave them all confidence. When she was dressed in her snowflake costume and came whirling away from the rest of the dancers on the tips of her toes, she was, in her imagination, indeed a snowflake, spinning, sailing, whirling, on every air current from heaven down to the earth.

When the time came and she could say, "In ten days my family will be here, Mother and Dad and Robbie and Uncle Jim," she was almost speechless with joy. She promised Marty that Uncle Jim would tell her about the time he shot the big bear that had owned the now famous tooth. She invited Miss Carey and Gertrude to go to dinner with her family the night before the pageant. She had got the swing of it at last. She had set her course and she was sailing.

CHAPTER 15

THE WEEK THAT followed the bishop's talk was the
beginning of a new life for Lisbeth Craig. She had
learned that the girls were separate and individual
like herself. She could no longer think of them as a
flock of sheep. There was Lexy Graham, who had
a guardian and whose fortune would be great when
she came of age; and Sally, who had no mother, but
a father and brother whom she adored. Anne's
father was in the diplomatic service and her brother
at school in England. Jane Trenton's family raised
oranges for the market, and Gail Hathaway's mother

was an artist and her father was a judge. They were all so different that Lisbeth wondered how she had ever thought of them as a collective pronoun. Even girls like Jinny Clarke and Leila Gordon, whom Lisbeth did not like at all, were different as could be. Jinny, the worst-behaved girl in school, was a professor's daughter! For the first time in her life Lisbeth began to notice people. She still felt separate, but she became aware that the others were separate also. She worked with renewed vigor in the rehearsals for the pageant and became again a part of the group who had leading roles.

When, at the end of the week, she received a telephone call from Uncle Jim, she was overjoyed. He told her that he and Robbie were coming to call on Saturday, a pre-party call, Uncle Jim said. He had already spoken to Miss Townsend and made arrangements to take Lisbeth and Gertrude out to dinner with him and Robbie. They were driving south for the football game and would stop at St. Anne's afterwards. Lisbeth rushed upstairs to find Gertrude.

The senior girls of St. Anne's roomed alone, and Gertrude's room at the end of the north ell was smaller than Lisbeth's, but she liked it better. There were more books on the shelf and the desk had room for notebooks and a typewriter. Gertrude was sorting her sheets of music when Lisbeth rushed up to the open door.

"Come in, Lisbeth," she invited, "and excuse the mess. Saturday's such a good day to straighten up the week's leftovers."

"Gertrude! Uncle Jim's coming—this evening! Robbie's coming too, and they want to take us out for dinner!" Lisbeth stood in the middle of the room, gazing rapturously at her friend.

"Oh, how nice!" Gertrude exclaimed. "I'm awfully glad I'm going to meet them before the pageant, Lisbeth." She looked up, and Lisbeth saw that a faint color had come to her cheeks. "I'm so dreadfully shy when I first meet people," she explained. "This will give me a chance to get over it before the party."

"They're awfully easy to get acquainted with," Lisbeth assured her. "Uncle Jim said we're going to a place near here where they serve wonderful squabs they raise themselves, but it's a plain place. We can wear the same clothes we wear to church."

"I've never eaten squab in church clothes," Gertrude laughed. "Or in any other kind of clothes, for that matter."

"We're going to have fun!" Lisbeth danced a little turn around the room. "Oh, Gertrude, I can't wait for the hours to pass. What shall I do in between?"

"Write a letter to somebody," Gertrude suggested. "When I start a letter, an hour or two passes before I know it."

Lisbeth went to her room and tried to write a letter to Mother and Dad. Suddenly in the middle of all her joy she was homesick. They were coming so soon, but the last days of waiting were longest. She began to think of Hermit Bay, and when the lunch bell sounded, she wandered out into the hall so full of conflicting emotions she wanted to cry. She met Sally and told her that Uncle Jim and Robbie were coming.

"I know how you feel," Sally said. "I love to have Daddy come to see me. But when he comes, I feel so sad I nearly die—but I'm happy, too. I know how it is."

"I don't know how I'll ever get through the afternoon," Lisbeth confided.

"Why not come and take a riding lesson?" Sally suggested. "The beginners are all allowed to ride out now, but I'll stay with you in the ring. Come on. It will be fun."

It was almost time to dress for dinner when Lisbeth got back to school. She took off the riding clothes she had borrowed from Sally and ran for the shower. She was glowing with the excitement of her first riding lesson and her blues had gone. She had barely finished dressing when Miss White came and told her that her uncle and her brother were in the reception room.

In the front hall Lisbeth paused for just a second, and then, instead of going around to the plebs' stairs, she dashed down St. George's Hill. As she reached the foot of the stairs, she met Gail Hathaway and Betty Gray just as they were starting up.

"Stop, pleb!" they ordered.

"I can't," Lisbeth cried. "I'll explain later!" and she rushed toward the reception room.

Miss Carey, on duty in the front hall, looked up and laughed. "You got caught, Lisbeth, but I think it was worth it. Betty and Gail just happened to be late coming back from town."

"I couldn't help it," Lisbeth said breathlessly. "Uncle Jim and Robbie are in there." She indicated the reception room door.

"I know," Miss Carey said. "Go on in. They're as eager to see you as you are to see them."

In another moment Lisbeth was in the reception room. Robbie and Uncle Jim were sitting on the

Victorian settee, looking polite and uncomfortable. They sprang up when she came in.

"There's my baby!" Uncle Jim exclaimed, lifting her off her feet as she ran into his arms.

"Uncle Jim! Robbie! Oh, I'm so glad to see you," she gasped. She hugged Robbie and he looked at her, shaking his head.

"Still my little wild girl under the skin," he said, grinning.

"Let me look at you," Uncle Jim said, taking her hands and standing off at arm's length. He looked at her so keenly that she felt he was seeing everything that had happened since she came to St. Anne's. "Is the sailing smooth?" he asked.

"Yes, with a fair breeze and everything," she told him. "It wasn't for a while, but it is now." She looked at both of them, at Robbie with his curly blond hair and Uncle Jim, wearing his clothes in that special way of his. "I wish they could all meet you, the girls, I mean," she said. "Can't you stay over—or have dinner here tonight?"

"We'd be terrified," Robbie declared.

"Hadn't we better take it in two easy lessons?" Uncle Jim asked. "You and little Miss Lee come out with us this evening. I've already told that pretty girl in the hall we're stealing you away."

"That's Miss Carey!" Lisbeth said. "She's my teacher-adviser."

"Bring her along," Uncle Jim suggested. "There's room for six in the car. Is there anybody else you'd like to bring?"

"I'll ask if we can take little Marty Evans. She's dying to meet you and hear firsthand how you shot the big bear."

"I'm beginning to feel like an uncle myself," Robbie remarked. "I've never been out with a car full of kids. Where's the child we're to take to the party?"

Lisbeth almost told him that Gertrude was not a child, but she stopped just in time. She would let him find out for himself. "She'll be down in a minute," she said. "Sit down and I'll see about Marty. We won't be long."

Miss Carey could not leave her hall duty until a few minutes before the bell chimed for dinner. She promised Lisbeth she would hurry and dress and join them in the reception room as soon as she could. After some hesitation, permission was given for Marty to go with them, and the three girls descended the plebs' stairs together. Little Marty clung to Lisbeth's arm, silent with awe at the prospect of meeting the man who had shot the bear with the big tooth. The bell had chimed and the hall was filled with girls on their way to the dining room.

Lisbeth heard her name and turned to find Jane and Gail behind her. "You're under arrest for traffic violation," Jane said, trying to keep a solemn face. "Gail saw you go down St. George's Hill."

"I'm guilty," Lisbeth admitted. "I just had to go the shortest way."

"You will be tried this evening and the verdict handed down in the morning," said Jane in a senatorial tone. "The patricians of South Hall will decide whether you're guilty or not."

When they went on, Lisbeth looked at Gertrude. "What shall I do?" she asked.

"They usually have a mock trial and sentence the pleb to do some funny thing or other," Gertrude told her. "It's a sort of test of your good nature."

"I'll let tomorrow take care of itself," Lisbeth said. "Tonight's going to be fun." With Marty holding on to her hand, she went jubilantly into the reception room.

Uncle Jim and Robbie stood up as the girls came in, and she presented them to her friends. Marty looked at Uncle Jim and then at Robbie. "You saw Mrs. Higgenbottom in real life, didn't you?"

Robbie's eyes were on Gertrude. "Mrs. Who?"

he asked, looking down at Marty. "Oh, yes," he went on, "I found my sister chatting with Mrs. Higgenbottom one evening last June."

"The Higgenbottoms are so well known that we expect the cubs to enroll at St. Anne's next term," Gertrude told him.

"I haven't had the pleasure of meeting them," Uncle Jim told Marty, "but I know a number of their relatives."

Marty laughed with delight. "Please tell me about the bears, Uncle Jim," she begged, as Miss Carey came in through the door.

Lisbeth had never seen Miss Carey look so pretty. She wore the dark suit and lacy blouse that Lisbeth had seen before, and her hat with the little veil was the one she wore every Sunday to church. Yet she looked different. She had a glow about her as she walked into the room. Uncle Jim straightened up and watched her.

"I hope I haven't kept you waiting too long," Miss Carey said.

Uncle Jim grinned at her. "It was hours," he said. "But it wasn't too long." Then he reached for Lisbeth's coat and held it for her. "Come on, baby," he said. "This is your party."

In her bed that night Lisbeth tried to put together all the thoughts and feelings that were spinning around inside her. All evening Uncle Jim had made her feel that the party was hers, that it was she entertaining him, instead of the other way around. Everyone had been gay all evening long. It had been a lovely party.

They had got back to school before time for lights out because of little Marty. But Lisbeth did not mind. Tomorrow night they were having the dress rehearsal for the whole pageant and she was looking forward to that. Besides, she would be seeing Uncle Jim and Robbie again in just three more days.

She sighed happily, thinking of Mother and Dad getting ready to fly south and of all of them there at St. Anne's to watch her dance in the pageant. She closed her eyes, thinking of Hermit Bay and her snowshoes standing beside the door, and of how Mother looked when she poured the tea by candlelight. Drowsily she wondered if Uncle Jim had meant it when he told Miss Carey that one of these days he was going to kidnap her and take her to see Hermit Bay. It seemed to her that Uncle Jim's broken heart was on the mend.

CHAPTER 16

THE PLANE DRONED through the dark of the morning and Lisbeth half drowsed in her seat across the aisle from Dad. At first they had all tried to keep on talking, because not nearly enough had been said, but gradually they had stopped trying to shout above the noise of the engines. Now everyone was half asleep.

Lisbeth smiled as she drowsed and let all the exciting and beautiful experiences of yesterday drift through her mind. All the unhappy memories had seemed to dissolve in the success of the Christmas pageant. She had been proud of St. Anne's and proud of her family when the girls crowded around to meet them.

She dozed off, and when she opened her eyes again there was light behind the pale overcast. All around the plane the snowy mountains leaned against the sky. Each familiar peak and island mountain was there, and the water down below was ruffled and streaked as though it had been laid on the landscape in brush strokes by an artist. Lisbeth looked across the aisle at Dad and smiled. Then suddenly there were tears in her eyes and she said, "Oh Daddy!" She wanted to tell him that this was what she had dreamed about at St. Anne's. She had longed for this wild, beautiful country with its wonderful feeling of peace, and now she could hardly bear these last few minutes of waiting to see Hermit Bay.

She could feel that the plane was losing altitude and she pressed her forehead against the window in her effort to see farther ahead. Then they were coming in over the long shoulder of the mountain and, at last, the bay was before them. She got a glimpse of the Narrow Arm, like a long silver finger pointing into the white forest, and she trembled in her excitement and eagerness to be there again in her skiff, to go immediately and reassure herself that nothing had changed.

When Dad shouted, "Fasten your safety belts, everybody!" Lisbeth felt blindly for the buckle, still keeping her eyes on the scene below. There was the cannery wharf with Ole and Doggie Dash running across it. She felt a lump in her throat. Then the plane bounced on the water and the spray was flying across her window. They bumped along and settled. When they reached the float, she saw Ole grab the wing of the plane, while the old dog ran from one window to the other, making little jumps with his front feet.

Feeling suddenly shy, Lisbeth hung back while Uncle Jim and Robbie and Mother got out. She came last, with Dad, her heart too full for words. Just as she got to the open door he gave her a squeeze. "You did a fine job of it, honey," he told her. "Keep your flags flying."

Halfway between laughter and tears, she made a funny little involuntary sound and they both laughed. She stepped down on the float and Doggie Dash made a bound for her. Ole looked at her, blushing bashfully as he greeted her, and she suddenly became aware of her city clothes. She dropped down and hid her face against Dash's sympathetic ear. She did not want to feel strange. She wanted to start right in where she had left off.

"He miss you somethin' awful," she heard Ole say. "When first you are gone, he come to stand every day on the dock and look down the bay."

Lisbeth gave her dog a hug and got to her feet. "You petted him, didn't you, Ole?" she asked. "And talked to him?"

"Oh, ve have long talks," Ole assured her heartily, as he fumbled with the many traveling bags.

Robbie was trying to carry all the bundles and the enormous turkey as well, and Uncle Jim came to Ole's rescue. Dad was asking the pilots to stay, but they looked thoughtfully up at the snow clouds and shook their heads. Lisbeth followed Mother up the gangplank, longing to get into her old clothes and take her skiff and head for the Narrow Arm. When she got on the dock, she started running for home, with Dash trotting happily at her heels. Looking toward the house, she could see blue smoke pouring out of both chimneys and she knew Long Paul was there.

As she came along the walk, she saw two deer standing on the front porch, ears forward, gazing at her. And there was Johnny the Buck in the snow in front of the house! Lisbeth stopped running. She walked on slowly, looking with pleading eyes at the deer. "Sue! Oh, Sue," she coaxed, as her pets shied away from her. "Johnny, you remember me, don't you?"

She did not expect young Susanna to remember her, but she could not bear it if Johnny the Buck and Faithful Sue had forgotten her completely. She stopped walking and talked to them and then went on, a step or two at a time. But Sue was nervous, and she walked away with Susanna to the farthest end of the porch.

On the verge of tears, Lisbeth stood where she was on the flat stones that led to the porch. Then, with a sudden rush, Billy the Third came bounding around the house. With a snort, he came straight for Lisbeth and gave her such a bump with his head that she almost fell over.

"Little wretch!" Lisbeth murmured, as she rubbed his head and scratched behind his ears. "*You* haven't changed a bit!"

Billy bounded up on the porch ahead of her, and then Sue came forward a few dainty steps and stood looking.

"Come on, Sue. Come on, my pretty," Lisbeth wheedled, as the doe came shyly on to nuzzle her fingers.

When Lisbeth entered the kitchen, Long Paul

turned away from the stove and they looked at each other for a moment in silence.

"They got you dressed up like a lady dude," Paul said finally.

"Not for long," Lisbeth retorted, heading for the stairs. "You'll see!"

At the door to the hall she stopped, holding her hat and gloves in her hand. "Paul," she asked hesitantly, "could you . . . would you . . . put my boat in? Please?"

They could hear voices and laughter down on the walk and a rush of sound as the deer all came plunging around to the rear of the house.

"I gotta go!" Paul said hurriedly, starting for the back door. "Ya. I put your boat in," he added as the door closed.

Lisbeth went bounding up the stairs and Dash took his old accustomed place at the bottom to wait for her.

When she came downstairs, clad in her old winter clothes, the feeling of strangeness that had haunted her was gone. She could hardly wait to get into her boat and really find Hermit Bay again. Everybody was gathered around the stove in the kitchen. The kettle had begun to steam and Mother already had cups on the table.

"Hadn't you better eat something before you start out?" she asked, as Lisbeth headed for the door.

"Let her go, Mother," Dad advised. "Eating is the pleasure of the old. She has other things to do."

"Why, Dad!" Mother laughed.

"Don't worry," Lisbeth called back to them, as she went through the house. "I'll eat with Long Paul and Ole."

As she ran past the cookhouse, where her friends had their winter quarters, she shouted to them to wait for her before they had their second coffee. Then on she went to the wharf and down the gangway to the float. Her red skiff was there, and she stood for a moment looking at it. Dash jumped in and took his place in the bow. Then Lisbeth cast off and picked up her oars. She rowed standing and facing forward, exultant and happy, as she headed out around the wharf. It was so good to feel the water on the blades again and hear the skiff slap the little scalloped waves that came running toward her. She lifted her face to the moist, cold air. Here, at last, was her own Hermit Bay, with winter on the beaches and snow lying lightly on the forest. The mountains towered upward to lose themselves in the gray overcast, and the head of the bay, drenched in blue shadow, seemed to stretch on forever.

After she had rounded the point of the Narrow Arm, Lisbeth sat on her crossboard and drifted with the tide. Before her the long finger of green sea water pointed into the frosty forest. There, at her left, stood the old cedar tree where she had watched the Higgenbottom family. Its great drooping branches were white with shining snow. If there were any tracks beneath it now, they had been made by wandering wolves. Somewhere, deep in the woods, the bears were drowsing the winter away in their holes. All around stood the forest, each tree shaped in white. In the brooding silence Lisbeth rowed on, gazing at the scene around her, so lovely, so pure, and so quiet. She had seen this place many times before, but she felt she had never known it as she knew it now.

A light gust of wind blew out of the mountains, ruffling the water and bringing with it a flurry of snowflakes. Ecstatically, Lisbeth watched the big white flakes as they tumbled this way and that through the shadowed air and vanished in the water without a trace. She saw them veil the mountains and sprinkle the tide-washed beach and deepen the white blanket that already covered the old hermit's cabin. She held up her hand and watched the snowflakes light one at a time on her wool glove. She thought that never, never in her whole life had the snow been so lovely.

At the head of the Arm a doe with her half-grown fawn came out of the alders and walked across the beach toward the hillside, unaware that anyone was watching. They came to a barrier of driftwood and, with a sudden flash of power and grace, the doe leapt over it. The fawn followed and together they disappeared in the trees.

Lisbeth gasped, and realized that she had been holding her breath. Then suddenly there were tears in her eyes. She had not lost her wilderness. She knew that now. But she had never felt like this before. She had never before been moved to tears when she saw a wild deer leap. She sat there, feeling the tiny cold kisses of the snowflakes on her face, feeling the closeness of the forest and the sea around her. Gradually, the peace and wonder and the inner joy that had been hers when she was a little girl grew within her. "Why, it's more," she murmured aloud. "Somehow, it's even more than it was before."

Hearing her voice, old Doggie Dash stood up and shook the snowflakes off his black coat. He looked at her hopefully. Lisbeth pulled her wool gloves higher on her wrists and started rowing. "Now we'll go," she told him. "We'll go home and have breakfast with Long Paul and Ole." At the word *home,* he sat down and banged his tail on the bottom boards and reached his nose in the air to sniff the wind.

Lisbeth rowed back with the snow flying over her head in the rising wind. She had found her wilderness again with its solitude and its peace—and something more. She rowed hard. She was in a hurry now to talk to Long Paul.

She found her friends in the big kitchen behind the mess hall. In the doorway, she ordered Dash to shake himself. Then she brushed the snow off her cap and jacket and crossed the room to hang them behind the stove. Long Paul sat with his chair tipped back against the wall, while Ole ladled sourdough flapjacks onto the top of the hot range.

"I was thinkin' you got stuck on a reef somewheres," Long Paul remarked.

Lisbeth stretched her hands out in the heat of the stove where Ole was concentrating on the flapjacks. "Not here," she answered. "But I nearly did at school."

There was a silence, and she could feel them waiting to hear what had happened to her and wondering how much she had changed.

"I tried to chart a course—like you said—but I

couldn't," she told them. "You can't chart a course there."

Long Paul nodded his head understandingly, and Ole deftly flipped the cakes and waited. They both looked so serious that she hastened to go on.

"I finally got under way," she assured them. "But I had to ride out an awful storm." She smiled at Ole. "I took your advice. Oh, I thought of you both so many times!"

Ole put the cakes on the table and set one aside to cool for Dash. They all sat down to eat. Little by little, Lisbeth told them all about St. Anne's. Then, shyly, she told them what she had found in the Narrow Arm.

"I was so afraid it would be changed," she said. "But it was even more . . . even more wonderful than I remembered it. I don't know just how," she went on, perplexed and trying to find a meaning. "I tried to remember how it was last winter before I knew for sure I was going away. . . ." She paused, looking to Long Paul for help.

He nodded his head again. "You was like a little mink then," he said. "Here was your woods an' your beach where everything yust *was*."

He fell silent, but they knew something else was

coming. Ole and Lisbeth waited while he pushed his chair back and filled his pipe.

"The little mink," he went on, "he take everything as he find it. He don't know no better. But you go away and then you learn it is from *here* you get the strength you need." He tapped his chest with his brown fist. "You grow up close with nature an' she give you strength."

They were silent again while Long Paul lit his pipe and Ole filled the coffee cups. It was a companionable silence, and in it Lisbeth knew that Long Paul was right.